Pasta, Poppy Fields and Pearls

Sophia Bar-Lev

ISBN: 1-4826-9539-1
ISBN-13: 9781482695397

Prologue
Florence, Italy 2010

Their laughter was contagious. Customers throughout the cafe stole furtive glances at the four women sitting at the corner table by the large window, sipping their cappuccinos and obviously relishing the exquisite Italian pastries called cannolis for which Cafe Toscana was famous. To even the most casual observer, it was clear that the women were thoroughly enjoying themselves and patrons of the cafe couldn't help but feel uplifted themselves in the atmosphere of happiness emanating from the corner table. Antonio, the head waiter, smiled from behind the ornate mahogany counter as he surveyed the pleasant scene before him. It was August, the height of tourist season, and the cafe was full.

Situated across the piazza from the historic City Hall of Florence, the cafe itself was a delightful place. The tables and chairs were antiques, the decor distinctively Italian with bright bold colors and locally made pottery. The cannolis were served on eye-catching hand painted plates which matched the tall mugs filled with the cafe's signature drink—frothy, steaming cappuccinos, the best in all of Florence. The food and beverages were delivered by smartly dressed waiters, meticulously trained. They weren't just waiters; they were performers demonstrating to their world of visitors the traditional hospitality of Tuscany, that northern region of Italy which attracts tourists by the thousands year after year. Florence, capital city of the northern region of Italy, is traditionally considered the birthplace of the Italian Renaissance. Its art and architecture are among the very finest of Europe.

But the four women at the corner table were not tourists. They lived in the countryside nearby and met twice a month at Cafe Toscana. They were all expatriates who had chosen Tuscany as their retirement haven. Two of them spoke passable Italian, "passable", that is, if you weren't a teacher of Italian; the other two were less adventurous; they stuck with their native English. They came from different locations, different careers, totally different backgrounds but they had one thing in common that had birthed and continued to strengthen their friendship.

The women loved Italy. More specifically, they loved Tuscany and the relaxed way of life they found there.

They often joked that the pasta and the poppies drew them to this locale. Vast fields of flame red poppies in the landscape were almost synonymous with Tuscany and all things Tuscan. In northern Italy's strong sunshine the poppies flourish and that same sun highlights their brilliant hue. Stunning against the lush greens of Tuscany's fields and bold when paired with bright yellow rapeseed flowers, poppies are one of the many glories of Tuscany and are often found in ceramic vases adorning Tuscan dining tables.

The heavy set one with the graying curly hair was Carmela. Born in Cuba in August of 1948, she was the daughter of a coffee farmer turned businessman and an expert seamstress mother who worked at home on an old Singer treadle machine, trying to earn a little extra money here and there to augment the family budget. And what a family it was. Carmela was the oldest of fourteen children and as such, it often fell to her to care for the younger ones while her mother sewed, cooked or was otherwise occupied with the constant work involved in managing such a large family.

Carmela's father was tall, handsome, rather quiet and a hard worker. Her mother was a fiery Latino, less than five feet tall. But what she lacked in height, she made up for in energy. She was a no nonsense kind of woman, practical to a fault and not given to much emotion. Her children meant everything to her and she labored unceasingly with them in mind, but her manner was a bit rough, bordering on harsh a little too often. The children feared as well as revered her.

Did they love her? Yes, Carmela says. They loved her but love and fear continually battled for supremacy in their interaction with 'Mamacita', as they called her.

It was Mamacita who decided that the family would have no future under Fidel Castro's regime. Without consulting her husband, she arranged to herd her children, all 14 of them, onto a fishing boat and escape to the "promised land" called Miami when Carmela was 16 and the youngest was 3 months old. Mamacita informed her husband of the plan just hours before their scheduled departure. He only asked, "Did you pack food for the children?" and followed her dutifully down the muddy road to the beach at midnight. For the rest of her life, Mamacita would say, "It was a miracle. *Madre de Dios*, what a terrible trip, but we made it." No surprise that Carmela never wanted to set foot on a boat again.

Opposite Carmela at the corner table was Paula Jean, blonde and blue-eyed, a southern belle if there ever was one. Paula Jean called Baton Rouge her hometown because she had been born there, but in reality, Mobile, Alabama is where she was raised and went to school. Paula Jean had the gentle and graceful ways of a southern lady, and her conversations were peppered with "Sir" and "Ma'am" to the great consternation of Carmela. One day some months earlier, the Cuban firecracker had had enough of being called "Ma'am."

The four of them had met at Paula Jean's apartment for lunch and to play cards for a couple of hours afterwards. Carmela had brought dessert, typical Spanish pastries called *'suspiros'* which she made herself. Offering the plate to Paula Jean, Carmela asked if she'd like one. "Yes, Ma'am," came the quick reply.

"Ay, Caramba!" Carmela shouted, following the outburst with a string of Spanish for which no one wanted a translation! Paula Jean turned white and her hands flew up to her face. Janet squealed at the outburst and Cecilia, ever the reserved Brit, began to hyperventilate as she muttered, "Oh dear, Oh dear, Oh dear."

Carmela slammed the plate down on the table, stood up, put her hands on her hips and towering over the seated Paula Jean said in a measured voice remarkably close to a growl, "If you call me 'Ma'am' one more time, I swear I'm going to slap you!"

Paula Jean's mouth dropped open as she stared in shock at her Latino friend. No one had ever spoken to her like that–ever. Cecilia and Janet, the other two members of the foursome, looked at each other with equally shocked expressions. Then all of a sudden, Carmela began to laugh ....and laugh ....and laugh. Then Janet's chin quivered and she began to laugh, somewhat nervously, unsure of why she was really laughing but unable to stop. Paula Jean looked at both of them and then at Cecilia, and in a completely untypical manner, pushed her chair back abruptly, stood up and looked Carmela right in the eye, her hands also firmly placed on her hips.

"ExxxxCUSE ME!" Paula Jean declared in a shrill voice. "What is YOUR problem–*Ma'am!*?"

Carmela stopped laughing and stared. The gentle southern lady could actually get ruffled! Amazing! None of them had ever seen that side of her before.

Collecting herself, Carmela said in a normal voice, "My problem is that in my country you don't ever want to be called 'Ma'am'. It's not nice, OK? You get it or do I have to spell it out?"

"Oh ... really?" Paula Jean replied, looking perplexed. "Well, where I come from, it's just the opposite. It's not nice to address any woman *without* calling her 'Ma'am'." They looked at each other for a few more seconds and then both of them burst into hilarious laughter with Janet and Cecilia joining in. They laughed until their sides ached. Paula Jean still called Carmela 'Ma'am' now and then after that and they would giggle every time.

Janet was the only Canadian in the group. She had grown up in a small town near Toronto but spent much of her life further west in the province of Alberta just outside the city of Edmonton. The long, cold winters and the heavy snows had given her more than enough reason to look for a milder climate for her retirement years. Tuscany for her was an escape from the brutal temperatures she'd lived with and she absolutely loved the green countryside, the flowers that grew wild everywhere and the fact that the wonderful city of Florence was close enough for her favorite hobby, shopping. But most of all, Florence was close enough for frequent visits to her three grandchildren. Five years earlier, her son had landed a job with an international law firm and was now a senior partner in the Florence office of Nelson, Nelson and Santorini, one of the most prestigious law firms in Europe. The young couple loved living in Florence and the grandchildren were flourishing there. It had been relatively easy for them to convince Janet to retire to Italy to be near them.

Cecilia hailed from London and was more British than the Queen, Carmela liked to say. But then, Carmela always had something to say, whether or not anyone cared. She was definitely the most colorful character among them.

Cecilia was 'proper', so very 'proper'. Her apartment was simply furnished but in good taste. Lunch at Cecilia's was always an "event". While Carmela and Janet were quite happy with every day stoneware dishes and discount store glassware, Cecilia was not. There was only one kind of dinnerware in Cecilia's cupboard–Royal Albert China in the traditional "Old Country

Roses" pattern. So very British! Paula Jean loved it but the other two constantly worried that they would break the delicate china.

No stainless flatware for Cecilia either. She proudly used her grandmother's sterling silver day in and day out, often quoting her venerable ancestor's favorite saying, "If you have it, use it. If you don't use it, give it to someone who will." Lunch at Cecilia's was definitely elegant, they all agreed, but they were secretly appalled at the lack of imagination and spice in her cooking. So bland, Carmela thought to herself; no wonder the British are so stiff. They need a few hot peppers to loosen them up, she told Janet after their second lunch at Cecilia's. In Carmela's opinion, British cooking hadn't improved one bit in the decades since she had spent a year studying in London. The food was appallingly tasteless then, too, for the Cuban student.

They look so relaxed, so happily engaged in the present moment, these four women drinking cappuccinos and savoring the creamy cannolis. To be sure, real life had collided, not always gently, with the dreams and plans of their youth but the casual observer at Cafe Toscana couldn't begin to imagine the kaleidoscope of experiences hidden behind the lovely smiles of four mature women basking in the magic of a sunny afternoon in Florence.

Was it just their love of Italy and all things Italian that continued to strengthen this vibrant friendship of theirs?

Or was there something else?

And by the way, did I mention that all of them loved pearls?

Chapter 1
The Way of the Determined

The solitary guest unlocking the door to Room 302 of the Savoy Hotel in London wondered at the dark-haired beauty who passed him in the hallway, pushing a cart laden with cleaning supplies, brilliant white towels and sheets and the amenities routinely distributed every morning by dutiful maids attired in crisp black and white uniforms with the renowned Savoy trademark embroidered on their aprons.

'Must be a student', he thought as he closed the door behind him. He smiled to himself, 'I should watch for that face at the theatre. She's beautiful.'

Oblivious to the fact that the distinguished gentleman she passed had noticed her, Carmela Mendes maneuvered the cart to one side of the hall, applied the brake to the wheels and exhaled a deep sigh. Another day just like yesterday, she thought. Cleaning bathrooms, sweeping floors, changing beds, and making sure that those wealthy enough to stay in this luxury hotel received all they expected by way of room service. That summed up her job. It wasn't an easy one but it paid the bills and kept her in school which is why she had come to London in the first place. A definite plus of this job was that she worked alone and once inside the rooms, there was no one to mind if she sang the melodies of her childhood in her native Spanish. Besides, the hotel provided housing for its staff as well as all their meals. She really had no reason to complain.

Carmela wasn't a complainer anyway. When someone commented on her easy disposition and optimistic outlook, she liked to say, "Who has time to complain when you're the oldest of fourteen children?"

Knocking first to make sure the room was empty, Carmela picked up the bucket filled with assorted cleaning supplies, grabbed the broom and mop and entered the room. The television had been left on and BBC was reporting on a war then being fought in the Middle East.

It was June 1967 and Carmela Mendes had arrived in London five months earlier, a few days shy of her 19th birthday. She came to study theatre, hoping it would lead to the fulfillment of her dream to become an actress and not just any actress, but an outstanding one. It was a dream she had carried in her heart since she was six when she saw her first live play in the company of her father in Havana. A very well performed though simple production, the drama had a profound impact on the six year old. She was transfixed by what was happening on the small stage of the local community hall which occasionally doubled as a theatre for live performances by local musicians, actors, and actresses. She had made up her young mind that very night to become an actress and never wavered in her determination.

She started 'working' at the age of nine, collecting bottles that could be turned in for pesos, going door to door in the neighborhood selling "jewelry" she fashioned herself from old buttons, old coins, bits of string and ribbon, colored beads or whatever else she could find, indoors or out, to use as materials for her initiative. Every peso was precious to the little girl and she would carefully hide them away in a small box she'd retrieved from a neighbor's trash barrel. She was quite proud of that box. It was gold foil on the outside and had originally been designed to hold perfume. It was spotlessly clean when she spied it thrown carelessly into the trash. Looking around quickly and seeing no one in sight, Carmela had grabbed the shiny treasure, tucked it under her sweater and hurried home to hide it far back under her bed so none of her siblings would find it.

Peso by peso she saved diligently until the small box could hold no more. Her next treasure chest was her father's discarded cigar box which was more than twice the size of her shiny gold box. She was sure that by the time it was overflowing with pesos, she would be very rich. She had lined it with a scrap of an exquisite lavender silk fabric, a small remnant from a dress her mother had superbly designed and sewn for the wife of a local politician. *Mamacita* was such an accomplished seamstress.

When Carmela was almost 11, a man by the name of Fidel Castro took control of the island nation and things began to change. Her father lost his ready smile and looked worried all the time. He worked just as hard as he had before the revolution but now it seemed they had less and less money to feed their growing family. *Mamacita* worked long hours at her sewing machine and earned fewer and fewer pesos. The boys were often short-tempered and got into fights which more often than not, Carmela was sent to break up. The younger children suffered from lack of attention and the home life of the Mendes brood was not as content as it had been in earlier years.

At the age of 14 she began her first real job. She wasn't thrilled with the work for it was more of what she did every day at home, but she was delighted with the weekly salary, meager though it was, for it exceeded her previous childhood earnings. Carmela washed dishes in the hot, steamy kitchen of *La Garida,* one of the most famous of Havana's paladars. *La Guarida* was the setting for several scenes in the Oscar nominated film "Fresa y Chocolate." Pictures of movie stars covered the walls and tables illuminated with dripping red candles created an ambience that recalled The Havana of the 1920's. The dining room was hidden away, up three long flights of poorly lighted stairs in an old beauty of a Havana historical building.

But for Carmela, the ambiance, the candles and the food were all irrelevant. What mattered was that she was earning money to realize her dream. She washed, she scrubbed, she swept the kitchen floor, and then she did it all over again, night after night until midnight or later, carefully noting the hours she had worked each week and double-checking her income to make sure not one minute of her efforts had gone unrecompensed. Every peso went into the old cigar box with the pretty lavender lining. Often when she placed her latest earnings into the cigar box, she would gaze longingly at the silk lining and dream of wearing dresses of beautiful fabrics just like that one. Carmela knew how to dream and had the common sense discipline needed to make dreams come true.

Though she routinely worked forty hours a week, her school work never suffered. Seated in her classroom promptly every morning at 8 am, she navigated her way successfully through mathematics, history, geography, language, music, and physical education until 3:30 each afternoon, when she rushed home to eat a light meal, change her clothes and report to work at *LaGuarida* by 4:00pm. She had been hired to work from 4 to 11 pm but most nights it was past midnight when she finally hung up her apron and started home. It was a grueling schedule for a 14 year old but Carmela continued at this pace for two years until the family fled Havana in search of a better life in the United States.

Arriving in Miami was a shock! How could a place so close to Havana be so vastly different, she wondered. Nicely dressed people spoke a funny language that Carmela didn't understand as they walked past beautiful shops with more clothes and shoes than she'd seen in her entire life. And the jewelry shops! She'd never seen such beautiful pearls. There were white ones and pink ones, grey ones and even black ones. She loved the pearls. So elegant, she thought. Surely, one day when she was a successful actress, she would buy herself the most beautiful pearl necklace she could find. Miami—what a magical place.

The family, at her mother's initiative, had crossed the open sea between the Cuban shore and the Florida coastline in the dead of night the last Wednesday of July, 1964. *Mamacita* had been organizing the escape for months and her diligent planning down to the smallest detail paid off. The seas were relatively calm during their crossing on a small fishing boat that reeked with the smell of decayed fish. Several of the children got violently ill, not from choppy waters but from the sickening odors of the wooden vessel. Carmela herself was sure they were all going to die and never be heard from again but when she dared to voice her fear, it was met with a sharp rebuke from *Mamacita* who informed her eldest in no uncertain terms that she was not allowed to even think of dying because there was too much work to be done when they arrived in Miami.

"Don't you know," she scolded Carmela, "that everyone in Miami is rich and we will also be rich and live in a nice house? Now stop moaning and think about what you are going to do in Miami."

Mamacita had thought of everything, except the possibility that they would be picked up by the US Coast Guard and turned back. That their escape should be anything less than totally successful was a concept completely foreign to *Mamacita's* way of thinking. Less than an hour before they were to go ashore at a predetermined remote beach where *Mamacita's* two brothers awaited them, a private yacht appeared on the horizon. However, the fisherman guiding them to freedom was no novice to smuggling refugees into Florida. He expertly manuevered the craft into an inlet, where Papa Mendes and the oldest boy, Carlos Jr., climbed over the edge of the boat into chest high water to help steer the boat closer to shore. Moments later, their benefactor shoved an inflated raft over the edge as Carmela and the next two oldest boys jumped into the water to steady the dinghy on either side. The fisherman passed the younger children down to Papa one by one and the baby Rosita who was 3 months old, he gently lowered into Carmela's arms who very carefully passed the infant to *Mamacita* seated in the center of the raft. Flashlights were waving a signal from the shoreline. Papa and the three boys firmly guided the raft in the direction of the lights while Carmela slogged along behind it.

They collapsed on dry ground just as the earliest hints of dawn began to chase away their cover of darkness. They turned back to wave their thanks to Manuel, the fisherman, but the dilapidated vessel had already disappeared.

Carmela's 16th birthday passed unnoticed that year, coming just a few days after their traumatic arrival in America. In less than a month, all the children were enrolled in school. Unable to speak a word of English, the first few weeks were difficult for them, but they quickly picked up the language, including some words from other students which they later had to delete from their vocabulary when *Mamacita* realized what her children were saying.

Carmela's dream ignited her determination and she entered North Miami Beach High School with her head held high though her mouth was dry and her hands sweaty with nervous anticipation. It was a relief to discover that many of her fellow students were also Spanish speaking. Some hailed from her native Cuba, having arrived a few months or a couple of years earlier. Others were from Puerto Rico, Costa Rica, Mexico and Nicaragua. Outside of class, they quickly reverted to their native tongue but within the classroom, English ruled. Carmela progressed rapidly and was soon tutoring the younger ones at home, as well as *Mamacita* who had no time to take English classes.

Life seemed to be taking shape for the Mendes family when another trauma blindsided the children. Papa had taken a job with a company that imported Spanish and Mexican foods and spices for the growing Hispanic population of south Florida. He began to travel to other cities in Florida to cultivate new clients for the company's imports. As the weeks went by, he seemed to be away from home longer and longer periods of time. It didn't take long for *Mamacita* to find evidence that confirmed her suspicions. There was another woman and *Mamacita* was not about to take that calmly.

The children returned from school on a Tuesday to find Papa's clothes in a heap outside the front door and their mother seething with rage. Every ounce of her Latino temper was loosed in a barrage of verbal warfare against Papa, who stood on the porch, immobile and looking utterly terrified.

In the end, Papa loaded his clothes into the dilapidated heap of metal that he called his car and drove off, after unsuccessfully pleading with his high strung wife to give him a chance to make things right. The children were devastated, especially Carmela who was very close to her father. She was angry and hurt. She understood perfectly what was going on and she was angry with her father for betraying the family but at the same time she was just as angry, if not more with *Mamacita*, as she blamed Papa's wanderings on her mother's harsh and dictatorial ways.

It was the last straw for the 18 year old. She was tired of being a second mother to all the younger ones, tired of listening to the arguing and eager to build what she envisioned as a "real" life. The night that Papa left with all his clothes was the night that Carmela decided she was also leaving. She just needed to figure out where to go and how to get there.

It didn't take long. Less than a week later, Carmela saw a notice posted on the school bulletin board which grabbed her attention. Auditions were to be held in Miami the following month for prospective students of the prestigious Academy of Theatre Arts and Dance in London, England. She read the information excitedly. There were scholarships available for those who qualified and living arrangements would be provided by the institution. Carmela wrote down the date and location of the auditions with determined intent to win a place in the new class of aspiring actors and actresses. Surely, she reasoned, as the oldest child of 14 in a family without a father, coupled with her very good academic record, she should be able to qualify for a scholarship. The important task at hand was to practice for the audition.

She approached the school's senior class advisor later that afternoon, who promptly gave Carmela all the information she needed in order to submit her application and prepare for the audition. Aware of Carmela's talents, the advisor strongly encouraged the young woman to prepare diligently, even offering to coach her as she practiced lines from a popular Broadway production which the advisor deemed a perfect choice to showcase Carmela's talents.

Carmela went to sleep happier that night than she'd been in quite some time.

The hard work paid off. Carmela placed first in the auditions, securing her spot in the next class at the Academy in London along with a full tuition scholarship. She was beside herself with joy and excitement. Her first thought at receiving the good news was to tell Papa. He would be so proud.

Carmela had made it her business to locate him within the first few days after he'd moved out of the family home. She assumed he wouldn't go far and she was right. He'd rented a room in a boarding house about a mile away, close to the office where he worked when he wasn't traveling around the state. Carmela visited him often and he was always visibly pleased to see his eldest daughter.

When she broke the news to him that she'd been awarded a full tuition scholarship for further study, he was elated beyond words. His proud smile faded, however, when she told him that the Academy of Theatre Arts and Dance was in London and she would be leaving for Europe in a few weeks.

"So far away?" he moaned. "When will I see you?" It was the first time Carmela saw tears well up in her Papa's eyes. She reached across the small table at the Cafe where they had met for coffee, squeezed his hand tightly, and with a lump in her own throat, she said, "Papa, it's only for a few years. I'll study hard and become a very good actress. Then I'll come back and I'll make a lot of money and you won't have to work so hard." Then she added, "And I'll buy a nice house and you'll come to live with me..." She paused and added wistfully, "I don't like it that you only have a room, Papa. I want you to come home and be with all of us again."

"I do, too, *querida*, I do, too." The sadness with which he whispered the words broke Carmela's heart. She struggled to hold back the tears. "I know, Papa. You should speak to *Mamacita* again. I think she's getting softer, Papa. I think she actually misses you."

Two days later, Papa came home, due in part to a trait which Carmela had inherited from *Mamacita*–a fiery determination to get what she wanted. After her coffee shop visit with Papa, Carmela had hurried home to announce her good fortune to *Mamacita*, who, upon hearing that her 'right hand' was going off to Europe, threw up her arms in her typically dramatic manner, rolled her eyes and after uttering several expletives reserved for the most upsetting of events, looked at her daughter and said, "You want to kill me, yes? You want I should be happy that you go off to such a school? Why can't you study here in Miami? Why can't you be a nurse? A teacher of English–you speak so well the English? What's the matter for you? Why you have to do something so crazy? Actress? *Ay caramba*–it's not a good life. Why I teach you all these years? For you to be actress? Why you do this to me?"

Carmela had expected just such a reaction and was prepared for it, or at least she thought so. She had to admit to herself that it was hard to see *Mamacita* so upset and she understood that behind all of the shouting and carrying on, in reality *Mamacita* was distraught at the thought of her daughter going so far away. She just stood there and listened, letting her mother vent all of her feelings. When she finally stopped, Carmela stepped over to her, put her hands on her mother's shoulders, looked down at her and said, "*Mamacita*, I have to live my own life. You had a dream–to bring us all to America so we could have a better life. I also have a dream. From my childhood, my dream is to be a great actress and I will do it. You will see." She paused and swallowed hard before continuing, "I will miss you, but I must go. It's a great opportunity for me that I would never have received if we were still in Cuba. You made this possible, *Mamacita*. Please be happy for me."

In a rare display of affection, *Mamacita* pulled her daughter close to her for a few moments, and said hoarsely, "Will be hard for me with you so far away." She pulled back and looked at Carmela intently and then, as only *Mamacita* could, issued a decree: "You go do this, then, but you do it the best. You make the dream come true, you understand me? You work hard, you push yourself, you make it very good. If you go, you make it good. You don't quit, you don't come back without good job. This is America–this where you can be anything you want. You do it good, Carmela. You do it good–then I be very proud."

In just as rare a display, Carmela grabbed her mother around the waist in a bear hug and lifted her off the ground. "I will, *Mamacita*. You'll see." She put her down and taking advantage of the good rapport of the moment, she added, "One more thing, *Mamacita*. Listen to me. It's time for Papa to come home."

Mamacita's eyes got very big, as her eyebrows arched up nearly to her hairline. "What you say?" she shrieked.

Carmela jumped in quickly. "Mama, it's not right that you continue to be angry and you don't forgive him. Papa is very sorry. He wants to come home and you must let him. The children need him. You need him, Mama, even if you don't want to admit it." Carmela was standing with her hands on her hips, feet slightly apart, fire in her eyes. The only time she ever addressed her mother as "Mama" instead of *Mamacita* was when she was determined about what she was saying, and *Mamacita* knew it.

The two of them glared at one another for a few tense moments. *Mamacita* was uncharacteristically quiet. Carmela stared.

"Madre de Dios," *Mamacita* mumbled softly after a couple of minutes. As if speaking to herself, she continued in an undertone, "First she tell me she go far away, then she tell me to bring Carlos home. Madre de Dios, too much for one day." She looked up then at Carmela, stared for a few more moments, then sighed heavily and turned and walked into the kitchen. Carmela followed her, pulled an apron off its peg and began chopping vegetables in silence. *Mamacita* continued muttering to herself while she mixed up a batch of corn bread, never looking at her daughter. The atmosphere in the kitchen was thick with tension. Nothing else was said between mother and daughter for the rest of the day.

The following afternoon when Carmela came home from school, Papa's car was in front of the house. Her heart skipped a beat as she ran up the two steps to the front door and burst through it. She stopped as she heard voices in the kitchen and as she listened, a smile spread across her face. Papa and *Mamacita* were actually speaking with each other in reasonably pleasant tones. She heard him say something about Mexico and pressed her ear closer to the door frame to listen. Papa was explaining that he'd been offered a good job, a promotion actually. The company he worked for wanted to open a new office in Mexico City and he would be the manager. It would pay well and life would be easier for them, he told *Mamacita*, if they started over in a new place. He pleaded with her to go with him. After a few minutes quiet conversation–so unlike *Mamacita's* usual manner–Carmela heard her agree to Papa's plan.

The next day Papa moved back home and he and *Mamacita* began making plans for the move to Mexico.

Now Carmela could go to London in peace. She fell asleep that night imagining what London would be like, what beautiful dresses she would wear on the stages of the theatre and just a bit anxious about venturing so far from her family.

In all her dreaming, she never imagined what awaited her.

Chapter 2
Love Comes Calling

He came often to sit by her at the dinner table where the off duty resident staff of the Savoy Hotel ate their hot meal every evening. Pedro hailed from Costa Rica and had arrived in London during Carmela's second year at the Academy. He worked in the kitchen of the Savoy and had spotted the dark haired Cuban during his first week on the premises. She was attractive to be sure, but it was more than that. Pedro found her fascinating. For all her beauty, she was down to earth and showed an interest in everyone around her. Unlike some of the drama students, she wasn't self-absorbed. Everything in her manner said that she cared deeply about other people and was genuinely interested in them. Pedro noticed that Carmela was hardly ever alone. Other employees sought her out regularly. She was fun to be with and she was a good listener, a quality universally appreciated by those who are lonely.

And who among them wasn't lonely from time to time? They were all foreign workers, far from home and family. Some came to study, as Carmela did. Others came simply to find work to help their families back in the "old country", as they called it.

That was Pedro's situation. His father had died three days before his 48th birthday from complications after an appendectomy, leaving his mother with nine children ranging in age from three to nineteen. Life was difficult in Costa Rica for the Santiago family and so after a few months, Pedro decided to take matters into his own hands. There was no future he could envision in his small village so he stuffed his few clothes in a faded blue backpack and made his way from the modest village of Tamarindo on the Pacific Coast to the bustling city of San Jose, the capital city where his mother's brother lived and worked.

Densely populated, San Jose is located almost exactly in the center of the country in a fertile valley in the Central America portion of the Andean Sierra Madre Mountain Range. The sheer beauty of the mountains in the distance along with the busy streets, called *calles*, was quite a change for the young man from the small coastal village. His uncle made the adjustment easier by taking his nephew on a walking tour of the city and securing a job for him within two days of his arrival. The year round sunny, spring like climate is perfect for growing coffee and some of the finest coffees in the world have been grown there for generations. Three days after arriving in the big city, Pedro reported for work at the Sanchez Amarinda plantation, one of the best in the area. It was an easy walk as the plantation was barely a mile from his new home with Tio Domingo and his family.

Pedro was quickly befriended by another laborer who also grew up along the coast but on the opposite side of the country. Tomas had been orphaned at the age of two when both his parents and a baby sister died in an epidemic of influenza. Tomas had also been quite ill but managed to survive under the watchful care of his maternal grandmother who raised the boy in her own home in the small town of Tortuguero on the Carribbean Sea. She was the only mother he remembered and he was devastated when she passed away two days after his 19th birthday. He'd come to San Jose, alone and with very little money, and had been at the plantation just two months before Pedro arrived. The two became fast friends and spent many of their evenings dreaming and making plans for a good life for themselves in the future.

It was hard work but the pleasant surroundings and a kindly foreman made for happy laborers. Lunch break at 12:30 each day was a routinely raucous time with 27 young men laughing and joking their way through the meal provided by their employer, after which they were given an hour for *siesta*, an absolute staple of Central American life. By 2:30 they were back in the fields where they worked til 6:30. Pedro returned to his uncle's home, knowing there would be a delicious evening meal waiting for him. Tia Lucia was an innovative and accomplished cook and he marveled at what she could create with simple ingredients, always flavored with the traditional spices that identify Spanish cooking. No two meals were alike but they always had one thing in common–plenty of rice and dark red beans to go along with the main dish. Why not? It was healthy and cheap and satisfied his eight cousins as well as Pedro and another young man whom Domingo and Lucia had taken into their home years earlier.

His name was Francisco and he was three years older than Pedro but you wouldn't know it at first glance. Francisco was mentally retarded and could only speak a few words. He smiled often and had a gentle and peaceful air about him. Everyone loved him and the younger children played with him as if he was their age. He would squeal with delight when 4 year old Franco would roll his shiny red ball across the floor to him, or 2 year old Alicia would climb all over him, laughing and tugging at him. He was one of those special souls that visit this world for a time and impact lives around them for good through their very simplicity.

About a month after his arrival, Pedro asked Tia Lucia one day how it was that Francisco came to live with them since he wasn't their child. Wiping her hands on her well worn red apron, she turned with a smile to Pedro and said, "He was a gift from heaven." Seeing Pedro's perplexed expression, she added, "He was left on our doorstep as a young infant, wrapped in a torn blanket. I found him in the morning, wide awake and shivering from the dampness." She sighed, "It happens sometimes, Pedro. Poor people–they don't know what to do with a child like this. They have no money, they have no help. Sometimes they put them in the garbage. Thank God, this one they put on my doorstep. He's a special one, Pedro."

"But, Tia Lucia, it's alot of work taking care of him. I watch you. And you have eight of your own," Pedro replied. "Aren't there places for children like him? You know, where the government takes care of them?"

Tia Lucia looked long into her nephew's eyes, so long he began to get uncomfortable. Then she gently put a hand on his shoulder and said quietly, "Pedro, I know about those places..." her voice broke slightly. "I grew up in one of them. They're not nice places." She paused and looked over at Francisco, happily playing on the floor like a toddler though he was in his mid-twenties. When she looked back at Pedro, she said, "All he needed was love. There is plenty of that in this house. This is where he belongs." At that, she turned and went back to the kitchen while Pedro looked after her with a new admiration for this aunt of his whom he'd never really known until now.

Some months later, Tio Domingo's eldest, Daniel, a strikingly handsome 24 year old, announced one evening at the dinner table that he had applied to go to university overseas. The noisy chatter at the table ceased as all eyes turned toward him and his mother gasped aloud. Tio Domingo's eyes narrowed as he looked questioningly at his firstborn but said nothing.

Clearing his throat and looking rather uneasy, Daniel returned his father's gaze and said, "Papa, don't worry about the money. There is this program for young people like me. I heard about it from Diego. They were talking about it at the university where he studies and he told me. In this program, they pay everything for me to go to school, a place to live, a job. I went to find the place today and a very nice man told me that he thinks I will qualify for their program." He paused, trying to read his father's expression.

Domingo nodded, "Go on."

Swallowing hard, Daniel rushed on, "I told him I want to study to be a doctor. Costa Rica needs doctors. I want to be a doctor for children. He said I would have to pass an examination which will be given in three weeks. If I pass, I will go to England."

Lucia pulled a handkerchief from her sleeve and dabbed her eyes. Domingo looked down at his plate. The younger children shifted in their chairs. Silence fell on the room like a thick blanket.

From the end of the table Pedro sighed a heavy sigh and then another. Some of the children looked at him, as did Daniel, waiting to hear what Pedro was about to say.

"Is there any possibility that I could ... I mean, do you think that maybe I ... ." he paused, and then blurted out, "I want to go with you, Daniel." Alicia wriggled out of her chair, climbed up on Pedro's lap and said, "I go, too" bobbing her curls up and down emphatically.

Her remark broke the tension as Lucia smiled and then two of the children giggled. A moment later, everyone was talking at once–

everyone except for Domingo. The patriarch sat quietly, looking around at his lively family.

"Papa?" Daniel addressed him tentatively.

Domingo looked at his eldest, sighed, and then gave him a faint smile and said, "I'm proud of you, Daniel. You will be a wonderful doctor." A solitary tear made its way slowly down his weathered face. It was a moment Daniel would never forget, a vote of confidence from the father he loved and admired, a strong but quiet man who rarely displayed his emotions.

Daniel and Pedro studied together every night, poring over the preparatory material Daniel had received from the Program Recruiter. It was more difficult for Pedro who had less of an educational background than Daniel, who willingly and happily tutored his cousin along, always encouraging, always urging him to believe in himself.

The morning after Daniel's announcement at the dinner table, Pedro had urged his friend, Tomas, to join him and his cousin in preparing for the exams. Tomas was reluctant. He knew nothing outside of Costa Rica and he spoke no English whatsoever. The challenge was too much for him and though sad at the thought of losing his best friend, he chose to stay with the familiar, however much it might limit his future.

Daniel and Pedro passed the examination and were chosen for the program. They would leave for Europe a month later, coincidentally on the first anniversary of Pedro's arrival in San Jose.

He gave notice at the plantation immediately in order to have two weeks free before his departure. One week he would spend visiting his mother and his siblings, taking them the money he had managed to save from his earnings at the plantation. The final week he would spend back in San Jose, shopping for suitable clothing for the trip while judiciously putting some money back to buy a warm jacket after arriving in London. He found it difficult to believe that it could get cold enough to need a heavy jacket, having spent all of his 22 years in a Caribbean climate, but heeding the advice of the Recruiter he planned ahead.

The transatlantic flight was traumatic for the young Costa Ricans who had never been more than a few miles from home throughout their lives and the city of London astounded them. However, exploring the metropolis would have to wait. They had only one day after arrival to recover from the long trip. The following morning was orientation, and they were told to report at 8 am promptly. Classes began that afternoon, which happened to be a Thursday. They were atypical classes, as each professor introduced the course, giving a brief overview and handing out materials. By 5 pm they were back in the room to which they'd been assigned, feeling completely overwhelmed, frightened and homesick.

Wisely, the program allowed them no time to brood or consider escaping. At 6 pm, the same day, nine of the students, Pedro among them, were taken to the Savoy Hotel to be briefed on the job which the program had arranged for them. Daniel would be working elsewhere, much to Pedro's chagrin.

Pedro's first introduction to the massive kitchen stunned him. He'd never seen anything like it. Stainless steel counters lined three of the walls and eight oversized ovens were stacked in pairs on the fourth wall. In the center was an enormous stainless steel island. He looked around utterly speechless until one of the chefs snapped his fingers in Pedro's face to get his attention. Embarrassed, Pedro started to apologize but the Oriental chef gave him a wide grin, slapped him on the back and said, "Iz OK. I was also *velly* shocked my first day. Come."

Within a week, Pedro had earned a reputation as the fastest food chopper on staff. He could whittle carrots, beets, green beans, onions and whatever else the chef needed chopped in record time and with amazing precision. The onions looked as if they'd been chopped by machine, each tiny piece perfectly square. Little did they know that Tia Lucia was responsible, for it was she who had taught him. It didn't take long for the Head Chef to begin teaching Pedro other skills required of those who prepared food for the guests of an elegant hotel like the Savoy where presentation was as important as taste.

It was on his first Sunday, just four days after his arrival that Pedro first caught sight of Carmela as she entered the staff cafeteria for the evening meal. She was simply dressed in a black skirt and pale yellow blouse, her curly dark hair pulled back behind her ears. "Carmela," a voice called, and Pedro watched as this girl who captured his attention turned in the direction of the sound. She smiled then and for Pedro, that smile lit up the whole room. He was smitten.

Being new to the Savoy kitchen, Pedro worked the morning shift and afterwards attended classes from noon to six pm, getting back to the Savoy each evening in time for the 7 pm staff dinner meal. By the third day he had managed to sit at the same table as the dark haired beauty. He watched her as much as he dared, trying not to be overly obvious. They had yet to meet but at least he knew her name, thanks to the anonymous person who called out to her that first night. Hearing her name had given him great hope–she had a Spanish name. Surely they would be able to communicate. *Madre de Dios*, he had thought. *What would I have done if she only spoke English!*

By the third week, Pedro summoned up the courage to invite Carmela to a movie at the university Student Center. She accepted and Pedro burst into the small room he shared with Daniel shouting, "Yes! She said Yes". Daniel looked up from the textbook he was reading, smiled broadly and then facetiously said, "Who said yes to what?" Pedro slapped his knee and flung himself down on the narrow bed, grinning from ear to ear.

The relationship flourished better than Pedro's studies, despite the fact that their respective schedules left little time for socializing. Classes, study and work at the Savoy consumed their time and their schedules at the hotel rarely coincided. Saturday night dates became the prize for completing another hectic week.

Well into her second year, Carmela was emerging as a talent to be reckoned with at the Academy, Daniel was doing exceptionally well in his pre-Med track but Pedro finished the first round with average results. Studying in English was more difficult for him than for Daniel but he was undaunted. He had reason to study, more than before. He came to England for an education in order to create a better life. By now he had already decided that his future had to include a certain dark haired Cuban who was the love of his life. He would overcome; he would improve his English and he would make her proud. He would work hard, get his degree, find a good job and make her his wife. He dreamed about watching her perform on the stages of Europe, and sitting in the audience gloating that she belonged to him; that after the curtain fell and the lights were dimmed, after the costumes came off and the theatre seats were empty, she would come out from backstage looking for him. They would go home together, and in due time, they would have children—beautiful children that all looked like her. As far as Pedro was concerned, there was no other option.

Carmela had entered the relationship cautiously but it didn't take long for Pedro to win her over. He was kind and thoughtful. It was obvious to the most casual observer that he was crazy about her. And he was funny. She enjoyed him. He made her laugh but they also had serious, heartfelt conversations. He became her best friend and for Carmela, that was every bit as important as romantic attraction. She often thought of *Mamacita* and Papa back in Miami. Letters were few and far between and she worried about them. Pedro was refreshing. He never raised his voice like *Mamacita*; he was more attentive to her than anyone had ever been in her life. *Is this real?* she sometimes asked herself. *Or is this a fairy tale? But he's such a prince.*

They'd been seeing each other for ten months when Carmela was summoned to the office of the Dean at the Academy one dreary Thursday afternoon. It had been raining for 12 straight days and the mood of many of the students and instructors matched the grey and dull atmosphere so when Carmela was greeted with a broad smile from the Dean, it piqued her curiousity.

"You sent for me, Sir?" she began. She'd never been summoned to his office before and was more than a bit intimidated and nervous.

"Yes, yes, come in. Please sit down here," Sir William Cuthright responded cheerily. He gestured toward the antique arm chair, upholstered in brown and gold paisley fabric with delicately carved wooden arms and legs. Carmela noted mentally that his entire office looked like a museum for antiques.

Being a no-nonsense kind of person, Sir Cuthright went straight to the point. "Surely you realize that you are one of our best students, Carmela. You have a natural talent for acting which our course of instruction has helped you develop and your progress has been remarkable, I must say. Your learn quickly and well and your performances are superb." He paused and cleared his throat, then went on.

"This office has been contacted by Nuovo Piccolo Theatre in Milan. The directors are looking for new talent, specifically for a young woman who would be suitable for a particular drama they are preparing to debut next year. You would be the ideal candidate and therefore, I want to recommend you forthwith and I hope you agree."

He paused as Carmela gasped and stared at him. "Really?" was all she could manage to whisper.

"Let me tell you a bit about the Theatre," he hurried on. "Have you heard of it? Are you familiar with it?" Not waiting for her reply, he continued, "When the theatre was first established in 1947, it became the first Italian stage after the tragic memories of the two world wars. Opening with a Gorki play, the theatre went on to a varied scope of Italian and international plays, aiming to affirm the concept of a "theatre for all" in the city of Milan. Inspired by its founders— Paolo Grassi and Giorgio Strehler–remarkable men, I must say, just remarkable—it evolved quickly into one of the well-known Milanese stages, rapidly enriching its theatrical palette with some contemporary interpretations of classic plays as well as modern works and even at times, light opera. It's a magnificent opportunity for you, Carmela, and I do hope you agree to go. I am confident that performing well in Milan will establish you as an international talent. Milan, my dear, is your door to the world of international theatre."

"I ... I don't know ... what about finishing my studies ... .how soon would I have to ... ."

He waved away her questions with a flourish of his hand, stood up and came around to the front of his desk. Carmela stood quickly, and as she did, Sir Cuthright put one hand on her shoulder, his piercing ice-blue eyes boring into Carmela's soul. He held her gaze silently for several long moments and then said softly, almost like a grandfather would address a beloved grandchild, "Carmela, my dear, this is a once in a lifetime opportunity. It will not come by again. You are ready, you can do this and you will succeed magnificently. Think about it if you must, but not for long. I need your answer by 9 o'clock tomorrow morning." He stepped back, smiled, gestured toward the office door and said, "Good day, Carmela."

Chapter 3
The Theatre of Life

"It all seems so long ago," mused Carmela, gazing for a long moment at one of the photographs on the wall. A smiling bride and her handsome groom looked back at her. "Can you believe I was ever that skinny?" she laughed.

She and Paula Jean stood on opposite sides of Carmela's sturdy work table, surrounded by mounds of fabric, and covered with bits of thread that clung to their cotton shirts like white lint on black wool. They were in the midst of another of Carmela's upholstery projects and since Paula Jean's easy chair was the object of transformation, she was drafted into helping.

Paula Jean knew nothing–absolutely *nothing*–about re-upholstering furniture. Truth be told, she barely knew how to thread a needle! She found the whole business just so, well, messy–and messy was something Paula Jean held in deep contempt. However, since it was *her* chair, she dared not breathe a word about her revulsion for the art of sewing and anything related to it. She endured–it took all of her Southern manners to do so.

To make the time of "helping", if you could call it that, go faster, Paula Jean got Carmela talking, admittedly an easy thing to do.

On previous visits to Carmela's home, Paula Jean had meandered around the living room perusing the gallery of family photos liberally displayed. She was awed by the large family, having always wished she'd had one. Paula Jean had only one sister and they weren't close. Now there's an understatement. Why, she couldn't even remember exactly where her sister lived, just somewhere in Oregon. Once a year she looked up the address to send a birthday card. That was the extent of their communication. Besides that, Paula Jean had no children. It was the greatest heartache of her life. She and her late husband had tried for years but it never happened and he was adamantly opposed to adoption. Having reached her late sixties, widowed and lonely, she had decided to do something really adventurous. She'd sold the home she and Jack had shared for more than 36 years, emptied her savings account, bought a plane ticket to Florence and moved! Just like that! Within three months, she had met Carmela, Janet and Cecilia and on the day marking four months since her arrival in Italy, she had written her best friend back in Alabama that she was never coming back. Now at seventy-one, she looked and acted younger than when she had arrived four years earlier.

"Time does seem to be speeding up, doesn't it?" she quipped to Carmela. "Jack's been gone nine years. Seems like yesterday in one way but in another way, I feel like I've been a widow forever. Do you feel like that?"

"Too often," Carmela responded. "We had such a good marriage, Pedro and I. Forty-one years we were married. Forty one years, six children, and fourteen grandchildren before he died, and more since. We had our hard times like everybody else, but I wish you could have heard Pedro laugh. When he laughed, everyone laughed. You couldn't help it. He had that kind of a laugh that was contagious. It was wonderful."

She paused, "You know, I didn't really appreciate what I had in the early years. We think life will last forever when we're young, don't we? But, oy–when he passed, what a loss." She shook here head and repeated wistfully, "What a loss."

"Tell me about Milan," Paula Jean interjected, lifting the mood. "What was it like to live there? I've never been. Florence charmed me and here I've stayed although I would like to see more of Italy one of these days."

Carmela laughed. "Milan? You want to know about Milan? Oy, what a city! Magnificent buildings, beautiful squares, theaters everywhere and always something to do. No one could be bored in Milan. No, no–never bored. A magical city. That's how I felt. Probably now I would feel differently if I went there but I was young, the city was exciting. Everything was an adventure. I loved it, every minute of it, except that I missed Pedro more than I wanted to acknowledge. To tell you the truth, I didn't admit to myself that I had fallen in love with him until I was in Milan. I missed him so much. I kept trying to talk myself out of it." Carmela giggled and looked sheepishly at Paula Jean. "You're going to laugh at me. You know what I used to do? I'd stand in front of the mirror and frown at myself and say—out loud mind you—'Carmela, get a grip. You are going to be a great actress; you don't need a boyfriend. You are not in love!! Think about your career.' I did that over and over again for about two weeks and finally gave up. It didn't work! I was in love and I couldn't talk myself out of it!"

"How su -weeet," Paul Jean said exaggerating her southern drawl. Both women exploded into gales of laughter.

Carmela went on to explain that she had lasted only two years at the Nuovo Piccolo Theatre. From the minute he learned that she was leaving London, Pedro had adopted an extreme austerity budget and saved enough money to buy a one way ticket to Milan in less than four months. He was waiting outside the theatre one afternoon when Carmela exited the backstage door to go home after an exceptionally long rehearsal. She nearly walked right past him without seeing him. He extended one arm right in front of her at the last minute and startled her. She was about to protest when her eyes met his, opened wide in total shock and just stared at him as if she were seeing a vision. He was grinning from ear to ear and finally said, "Well, are you going to welcome me to Milan?"

"Pedro!" she squealed. "What are you....how did you...oh, my God, I've missed you." She threw herself into his open arms as he smothered her with kisses, saying over and over again, "Don't you ever leave me again. Don't you ever leave me again."

She didn't.

They were married the following week in a civil ceremony, promising each other that they would have a "real" wedding back in Mexico as soon as Carmela completed her contract with the theatre. Pedro was hired by the theatre as a stage hand two days after arriving and worked there until they left for Mexico nineteen months later. By then,

Carmela was pregnant with their first child.

Readjusting to Mexican life proved more of a challenge than Carmela expected. Nearly four years in Europe had left its impact.

Pedro found it rather similar to his early life in Costa Rica except that Mexico City was enormous compared to his native village. However these were minor considerations for the young couple. They were happy, they were together, their first child was about to be born, her family was thrilled to have them back, her father was delirious over the prospect of becoming a grandfather and *Mamacita* was–well, *Mamacita* was–as always–*Mamacita*, bossy, independent, a bit brusque and even more opinionated, if one could imagine that, but no one doubted her love, certainly not Carmela. After all, they were cut from the same cloth. The years of separation had given Carmela a fresh perspective on her *Mamacita* and the two of them grew closer, albeit with the occasional emotional eruption.

Five more children followed in the next seven years. Pedro worked in a local factory, advancing in a short time to a supervisory position and within three years was a department manager with a small office of his own. Meanwhile, he also went to university classes two evenings a week.

Universidad Nacional Autónoma de México, founded in 1910, had developed into a prestigious institution of higher learning by the time Pedro became a student there in the late 1960's. Since he was a child, Pedro had dreamed of being a doctor but during his early life it was no more than that–an impossible dream for a poor orphan from a small village in Costa Rica. For Carmela, no dream was impossible and once she knew that her husband's real desire was to study medicine, she set about doing everything possible to see to it that he realized his dream. More than busy with six young children, Carmela became the prototype of the 'Super Mom.' She was highly organized, extremely efficient and demanded the same from the children. Each child had their own chores beginning with very simple ones like dressing themselves at the age of three. The older ones helped the younger ones and the household ran like a well-oiled machine, humming along with constant high energy activity which Carmela's sister, Iris, described as "utterly chaotic peace."

Pedro completed his pre-Med degree in five years, studying part time, working full time and still remaining very involved in the lives of his children. Carmela had become an expert seamstress, making all the children's clothing as well as her own, and marketing her skills locally to help support the family while Pedro studied. For his graduation, Carmela fashioned lovely smocked dresses in a soft shade of lavender for the three girls and shirts for the three boys in a complimentary shade of purple. For herself, Carmela had designed and sewn an exquisite dress of deep purple with ivory buttons down the front. Pedro whistled when he saw her emerge from their bedroom, ready to leave for the graduation. "My beautiful Carmela!" he exclaimed, as he picked her up and swung her around. "It's good thing you belong to me or I would be so jealous if you were someone else's wife!"

"I'll never forget that day," Carmela said to Paula Jean. "You can't imagine the joy on Pedro's face when he held the degree in his hands. Even after all the hard work he couldn't believe he was actually a university graduate. As for me, I was so proud. My Pedro was well on his way to becoming a doctor. It was just wonderful."

Paula Jean glanced at her watch. "I want to hear more about Pedro, but it's nearly five o'clock. Do you want to call it a day?"

"I suppose we should. I don't know if we did more talking or more upholstering but we had fun anyway. We can work on this chair again tomorrow if you want."

"Sounds like a plan to me," Paula Jean responded. "Oh, wait a minute. Tomorrow's lunch day and it's my turn." The four women routinely met every Thursday for lunch, each of them alternately hosting the group.

"Well, then, tomorrow's lunch certainly takes priority! The chair can wait," Carmela declared. "Eating's the best thing we girls do—after talking, that is," she chuckled.

Paula Jean grinned then bent down to pick up scraps of fabric that had fallen on the floor. Straightening up she turned toward Carmela and opened her mouth to say something, then closed it again and stared out the window for a few moments.

"Yoo-hoo, dream girl," chirped Carmela. "Earth calling Paula Jean."

"Sorry," came the quick answer. "Uh...can I help you put all these things away?"

Carmela waved her off. "No need. I got it. Do you want a cup of tea before you go?"

"No, no, thanks," Paula Jean replied. "I'd best be going. Lots to do for tomorrow's lunch." Brightening up, she continued, "I'm trying another new recipe. Bring your appetite!"

Grabbing her purse from the sofa, Paula Jean gave Carmela a quick hug and was gone.

Chapter 4
Ferko Shows Up

The midmorning sun was casting jewel tone shadows across Paula Jean's dining table as its rays played off the stained glass window panel on the eastern wall of the spacious room. Though it was only 10 am and the others wouldn't arrive for another hour or more, the table was already set and in typical southern style, beautifully decorated with small vases of multi-colored wildflowers cut that morning from the garden area behind the house.

Her china had come with her from Alabama, an heirloom set that had belonged to her grandmother. Plates with a dainty flowered border in shades of pink and burgundy were tastefully arranged on deep burgundy place mats and the crystal goblets sparkled–of course! This was southern hospitality on parade.

On arrival in Tuscany, Paula Jean had stumbled onto a charming country house in need of a creative woman's touch. She had taken on the project with gusto and after a full year of renovations and repairs, Paula Jean's home was lovely. A combination of Italian country with old-fashioned Southern elegance rendered it worthy of being chosen as a Better Homes & Gardens' feature though it never was. The magazine didn't reach quite as far as Tuscany when looking for publication worthy homes.

The garden added even more to its charm. Completely overgrown when she bought the place, Paula Jean had described it as a 'tangled jungle' in a letter to her friend, Delia, back in Mobile.

Elaborate Renaissance gardens with carefully manicured shrubs and stone walkways had been trademarks of the Tuscan countryside in days gone by. In more modern times, however, a new feeling of rustic innovation emerged making it seem as though for Tuscans, nothing is more modern than the past. Revived interest in 'the way things used to be' had produced a trend towards fusing past and present, formal and informal in the modern outdoor space today's Tuscan gardener creates.

Paula Jean took her cue from area homes she admired, combining generous sections of local wild flowers with a more structured and formal garden area close to the house, complete with typical stone benches and a picnic table shaded by a trellised grape vine along the south wall of the property. The garden was stunning, a fitting tribute to an avid gardener such as Paula Jean had been all of her life.

The house itself boasted large windows in every room. Her choice of an earth colors palette was perfect making each room blend seamlessly with the landscape beyond as she limited window treatments to simple but elegant valances to allow for maximum light as well as beautiful views in every direction.

Satisfied that the dining table was company ready, she made a quick sweep of the rest of the room before returning to the kitchen. Dainty sandwiches were dotted with artistic garnishes, the potato salad–Paula Jean's secret recipe and a favorite among the friends–was all the more appealing in the gleaming crystal bowl, another antique inherited from her grandmother. The results of her 'new' recipe, a strawberry-walnut-quinoa salad, was displayed in an heirloom bowl that was part of her grandmother's set of china.

The sound of a car making its way up the curved driveway distracted Paula Jean from the last minute kitchen clean-up. Glancing at the clock, she frowned. It was early and she wasn't quite ready. God forbid, any of her friends should arrive before she was properly dressed and her makeup applied. That would never do!

Darting into her bedroom at the end of the short hallway, she had just pulled her new skirt from the armoire when the doorbell rang. "Oh, no," she muttered, hesitating as she looked back down the hall. "If that's Carmela," she mused to herself, "she can just wait a minute while I change."

The doorbell rang again as Paula Jean fumbled with the buttons on her crisp white linen blouse. "Oh drats,' she mumbled, pulling the new lavender skirt over her head as she walked towards the door. Stealing a glance in the entrance hall mirror, and shaking her head in dismay, she opened the door and said, "Why are you so....?"

Her words hung limp in the still, humid air as her mouth dropped open. Her eyes widened. Stunned, she simply stared. So did he.

Moments passed in silence between them. Finally, he quietly said, "Paula Jean...may I come in?"

Completely flustered, her mouth dry and her hands trembling, Paula Jean said nothing. She just stood there, staring.

"May I come in?" he asked again. Shaking her head as if to bring herself back to reality, she nodded and stepped back a little so he could enter.

"Ferko," she whispered. "How did you ....?" Her breathing was uneven as she continued, "Why..."

The ticking of the antique grandfather clock marked the passing seconds. Ferko looked down at the floor and Paula Jean struggled to recover from the shock.

Lifting his head, he locked her eyes with his in a penetrating gaze. "Paula," he breathed softly. "So many years... but I never forgot."

Paula Jean squirmed nervously. He reached out a hand. She didn't take it.

"What about you?" he asked. "Did you forget?"

There was no response.

"Was I wrong to come, sweet pea?" he tilted his head, inquiring.

Her heart lurched at hearing the long forgotten term of endearment. Paula Jean let out a very deep sigh. And then another.

"Ferko," she said, her voice barely audible. "I'm shocked...um, I'm stunned. I don't know what to say. I had no idea..." She let out another deep sigh. "Um, please, be seated." She gestured towards the overstuffed chair.

"What are you doing in Italy?" she continued. "And how in the world did you locate me?"

Relaxing slightly, Ferko leaned back in the chair. "You weren't so hard to find, my dear," he replied with a feeble smile. "Not difficult at all."

The telephone rang and Paula Jean jumped to answer it, welcoming the opportunity to flee into the kitchen for a moment. She leaned heavily on the counter as she nearly shouted "Hello" .

"Are you all right?" Janet's voice clearly expressed concern, even alarm.

"Yes, yes...well, not exactly...um, yes, I'm all right, just a bit surprised, that's all," Paula Jean replied. "I had no idea...it's such a shock...I don't know what to say ... "

Janet broke in, "Paula Jean, what in the world is going on? You're not making any sense."

"I'm sorry. Listen, I've got to go. You are still coming for lunch, aren't you? Please say you're coming."

"Of course, I'm coming," Janet answered. "I was just calling to see if you needed me to bring anything."

"No, no, just yourself. Just give me a few more minutes to get myself together," Paula Jean said quickly. "I'm fine-- really I am. Just a bit shocked. I'll explain later.

Come anytime. You can come now if you'd like."

"On my way," came the prompt reply.

Hanging up the phone, Paula Jean held onto the counter for a few more moments, trying to pull herself together. She really didn't know how she felt. All she knew was that she needed to get rid of Ferko before Janet or any of the others showed up.

Smoothing her skirt and running her fingers through her silver hair, she took another deep breath and walked back into the living room. Ferko quickly stood up, his European upbringing not forgotten.

"Please, sit," Paula Jean gestured. He looked at her expectantly.

"Ferko," she began, "it's very nice to see you but... I hope you understand... this comes as quite a shock to me. It's been a very long time. "

"Fifty years and 9 months to be exact," Ferko interjected.

Paula Jean's eyes widened and her jaw dropped. "You've kept track ... ?"she inquired disbelieving. Shifting in her seat, she remarked, "Um...and you've hardly changed–amazing." Ferko smiled broadly. "Neither have you," he replied.

Ignoring the comment, Paula Jean continued, "I suppose we have a lot of catching up to do, but I must tell you this is not a good time. I have guests coming for lunch today and I need to...."

Ferko interrupted, "It's OK, Paula. I realize that I have burst back into your life with no warning and no invitation. I'm sorry. It was insensitive of me. When I discovered your exact location, I was so eager to see you that I didn't stop to think. I just came. I apologize." He paused, then added, "May I come to see you–or perhaps take you out for dinner... later? Or tomorrow? Whenever you'd like?"

"Yeeess," Paula Jean replied slowly in her southern drawl. "Tomorrow might be OK. Will you call me first?"

"Gladly," he grinned, "as long as you'll give me your phone number." He winked playfully.

Paula Jean chuckled slightly, the first hint of a relaxed moment since Ferko had appeared at her door. He punched the numbers into his cell phone and stood to leave. For a brief moment, they stood looking at each other a bit awkwardly, then Paula Jean quickly stepped forward and Ferko followed. She opened the door wide and smiled politely. Ferko extended his hand again.

This time she took it and in that split second was transported back fifty years and nine months. The feeling completely startled her. Seeing her reaction, Ferko leaned over and kissed her ever so lightly on the cheek then made a quick exit. He turned back to wave as he unlocked his car. She stood in the doorway watching as he maneuvered his blue BMW carefully away from the flower beds that flanked the driveway and disappeared through the trees that gave her home its wonderful privacy.

Paula Jean was in a daze as she made her way back to her bathroom. She tried unsuccessfully to apply her makeup and ended up just running a comb through her hair, muttering to herself, "I'm seventy-one years old for heaven's sake. What is wrong with me?"

Loud knocking snapped her out of her bewilderment. Janet burst through the door without waiting for Paula Jean to open it and called out in a tone remarkably like that of a mother looking for a lost child. "Where are you?" she demanded.

"Right here," Paula Jean answered weakly, coming out of the bedroom toward the front door.

"What happened to you?" Janet exclaimed. "You look awful."

"Thanks a lot," Paula Jean half-smiled in return. "I just couldn't get my makeup on."

Janet grabbed her arm, pulled her into the living room and sat her down on the brocade sofa. "What do you mean you couldn't get your makeup on? Are you ill?

There's no such thing as Paula Jean Jackson not getting her makeup on? What is WRONG with you?!? What happened?"

Just then the doorbell rang. Cecilia and Carmela traipsed in, took one look at Paula Jean and then at Janet and echoed Janet's words. "What in the world has happened?" they chimed together, staring at the two women on the sofa.

"It's a long story," Paula Jean began, "something I....." She dropped her head into her hands.

Carmela, Cecilia and Janet looked at each other quizzically, none of them sure what to do next. They had never seen Paula Jean like this.

Carmela stepped closer and crouched down in front of Paula Jean. "Whatever's happened, Paula Jean. We're here for you—if you want us to be." She paused, then asked quietly, "Do you need some time alone?"

"No, no," Paula Jean replied emotionally. "No, stay, please stay. Lunch is ready. The last thing I want you to do is leave! I just need to pull myself together. Let's have lunch." Then looking up at her three friends, Paula Jean sighed and continued, "Honestly I'd like to talk with all of you... if you have time.. this afternoon. But let's eat first."

She stood, looked at each of her friends for a moment then turned toward the dining room. The others followed her casting curious glances at each other behind her back.

Chapter 5
The Budapest Connection

"It all began in Budapest," Paula Jean began, "some 50 years ago."

Having finished lunch, the four women were now comfortably seated outdoors on the shaded patio. Four freshly prepared cups of cappuccino in exquisite china mugs and a crystal platter with Paula Jean's homemade signature cupcakes were artistically placed on the wrought iron and glass table which was covered with a starched white linen tablecloth.

"Budapest?" Carmela asked with one eyebrow raised. "I never knew you went to Budapest."

Paul Jean smiled weakly. "Like I said, I never talked about it."

"Talked about what?" Janet asked in her matter of fact style.

Cecilia nudged her as she gave Janet the famous 'Cecilia look' which meant *'hush already!'* Gently rebuked without a spoken word, Janet good-naturedly helped herself to a cupcake and leaned back in her chair.

"My parents took me to Europe for my 21st birthday," Paula Jean took up the narrative. "It was something they'd promised me when I was 16. I didn't realize until later that they had saved for years to make the trip possible. Among my circle of friends in Mobile in 1969, most of whom had never been any further than New Orleans, it was a really big deal that we were going to Europe.

"My Dad booked us on a transatlantic cruise from New York to England. It was a French line that doesn't even exist today and though we thought the ship was magnificent, it was nothing like the cruise ships of nowadays. We drove our old Chevy from Mobile to New York, stopping along the way to visit relatives in Virginia and reached New York the day we were to board the oceanliner.

It was very exciting as we set sail. I stood on deck with my parents watching the skyline of New York get smaller and smaller, thinking how fortunate I was to have such a great opportunity. How I wished my best friend back in Mobile, could have come with us. She would have loved it."

"Do you mean Delia? Your friend you talk about?" interrupted Cecilia.

"Yes, I so wanted her to go. I even asked her parents to let her go with us but they said they couldn't afford it," Paula Jean replied.

Carmela interjected, "Let's get back to the story already–I'm dying of curiosity."

With a faint smile, Paula Jean took up the narrative.

"We spent the first week in London, then went on to Paris, Amsterdam and Brussels. By the end of the third week, we arrived in Berlin for 4 days, then on to Prague for another 4 days. About the middle of the fifth week, we arrived in Budapest. I was feeling very European by then," Paula Jean chuckled. "I loved the ambiance of the great cities of Europe and the architecture mesmerized me. I couldn't get enough of seeing historical monuments and palatial government buildings. It was all so amazing to a girl from Alabama!"

"You remind me of how I felt when I arrived in London to study," Carmela interjected, reaching forward for another cupcake. "By the way, these cupcakes are fantastic."

Paula Jean acknowledged the compliment with softly spoken, 'Thanks' and returned to her story.

"My mother took a great liking to the European style coffee shops, something we didn't have in Mobile in those days. We couldn't afford to eat our meals there but every day, Dad, Mother and I would have an afternoon coffee and small piece of cake at one or other of the Cafes. It became a ritual. Dad would order one piece of cake and ask for two extra plates and forks. Each day we'd try a different cake. It was heavenly."

"Is that where you got the recipes for your cupcakes?" Cecilia asked. Paula Jean's cupcakes were the most delicious any of the women had ever tasted. There was something different about them, some hidden ingredient that Paula Jean guarded jealously.

"Not really," Paula Jean replied, "though I did learn a few things about baking during that trip, especially in Budapest."

Shifting uneasily in her chair, she continued, "We'd been there two days when someone told us about a very famous coffee shop that we'd not yet visited. The Gerbeaud was a grand old place, quite famous in European circles, having been in business since 1858. I must admit we'd never heard of it before but after our first visit we were addicted. You should have seen this place—damask draperies, crystal chandeliers, velvet chairs with carved wood tables and lovely paintings on the walls. It was sooo elegant. I felt like a princess when I ate there."

Suddenly, Paula Jean's face darkened and she bit her lip. She looked away and stared blankly. The women looked at her and then each other. No one said a word.

After several minutes, she turned back at her friends and said simply, "This is where the story gets painful."

Wisely, the three women maintained their silence and waited. Janet sipped her cappuccino. Carmela finished off her cupcake and Cecilia fiddled with her napkin. The distant hum of bees seeking nectar from the many flowers in Paula Jean's garden harmonized with the chirping of tiny sparrows in the trees surrounding the house.

"At the Gerbeaud," Paula Jean picked up the story after what seemed an eternity to the others, "there was a waiter, a young Hungarian, very handsome. He served our table the first day we were there. When we went back the next day, I made sure we sat in the same area. He was very attractive, very polite and I could tell he was noticing me as much as I was noticing him. After our second visit to the Gerbeaud, he asked my Dad if I might be allowed to take a walk with him along the riverbank after he got off work at 10 pm. Frankly I was shocked when my Dad gave his approval, but I was also pleased. I liked him. I liked him a lot.

That evening, he came for me at the hotel and escorted me to the promenade along the Danube. We walked leisurely for the next two hours, getting to know each other.

He was a student at the Franz Liszt Academy of Music and worked at the café after hours. He lived in a very small rented room and only once every two months, he told me, was he able to take the train to his hometown of Pecs in southwest Hungary to visit his parents and younger sister. Pecs was a smaller city than Budapest, he explained, but a city rich in musical history. He was very proud of that.

"Oh, I don't know why I'm giving you all this detail..."Paula Jean shook her head.

"It's OK," Cecilia remarked. "Just tell it like you want to."

"The next night we went out walking again, "Paula Jean carried on, "and when he brought me back to the hotel, under the oil lamp by the front entrance, we kissed. It was my first ever kiss and I was completely smitten. So was he.

"Mother sensed it as soon as I reached the room and looked at me curiously but said nothing. It wasn't difficult to see what she was thinking, however. I was relieved that my Dad was already asleep. I really didn't want to see him just then.

"We had two more days in Budapest and I longed to spend every minute I could with Ferko. Oh, did I tell you that was his name? Ferko? It's Hungarian for Francis." She paused and looked down.

Aware that this narrative was leading up to something important, Carmela said, "Go on, Paula Jean. "

"The third night he asked if I'd been to the Royal Palace on the Buda side of the river. I acknowledged that we had, but that I would love to go back and sit by the fountain and the perfectly manicured gardens. We made our way across the Chain Bridge and climbed the dozens and dozens of steps to the top. Ferko told me there had been a railway that carried people up to the top but it was destroyed in World War II and was yet to be rebuilt.

"Anyway, we made our way to the Fountain and the gardens, found a bench and sat down to rest after our climb. Two other couples walked by, hand in hand, talking softly, and then we were alone."

Paula Jean took a deep breath and then looked at each of her friends, tears brimming in her eyes and said, "What I'm about to tell you, no one has ever known. It's been my secret for fifty years." Unconsciously, each of the women leaned forward.

"Ferko and I made love that night, under the stars, alone in a secluded spot in the gardens behind the Royal Palace on top of Buda hill." The tears spilled over and slid down her face as her voice broke. Several moments passed. "He said he wanted to marry me and pleaded with me not to leave Budapest the next day. I was madly in love with him by then as he was with me. And somehow in my heart, I knew it wasn't just infatuation. I felt we were meant for each other. He wanted to approach my Dad the next morning to ask for my hand in marriage. I was frightened. I knew my Dad would think it was just a fleeting infatuation. Dad was the logical, engineer type.

"We got back to the hotel well after midnight. I couldn't sleep. I was torn with such conflicting emotions. I had never been with a man before and on the one hand I was horrified that I surrendered my virginity to a man I'd met just three days earlier. On the other hand, it felt so right though it flew in the face of everything I had ever been taught. I was a confused and conflicted young woman, but I was very much in love.

"True to his word, Ferko arrived at our hotel the next morning while we were at breakfast in the hotel dining room. He joined us there and after my father finished eating, he asked if he could speak with him privately. Mother looked questioningly at me as the two men left the table. I looked down and said nothing.

"It didn't take long. My father returned to the table minutes later and abruptly announced that we needed to pack and make ready to go on to Venice. He made no mention of his conversation with Ferko but his look said it all. I was devastated." Paula Jean sighed as she dabbed her eyes with a napkin.

"Mother and I returned to our room and packed the suitcases while my Dad went to the reception desk to check us out of the hotel, a day early. Within two hours, we were on a train to Venice. Everytime I glanced at my mother, she was watching me but would turn away as soon as my eyes met hers. I kept waiting for her to say something–anything–but nothing. I wanted to plead with her to help me, to understand me, but I knew she wouldn't. Father said nothing throughout the trip and I didn't dare ask. My father was an imposing man and I loved him but I was also very intimidated by him.

At one point during the train trip, I opened my purse to get my handkerchief and saw a crumpled up piece of paper inserted into the inside pocket. I knew it had to have been put there by Ferko. I wondered how he had managed to do it. I was very careful not to react and closed the purse. My heart was pounding and it took some effort to breath normally but I was determined that my Dad should not discover that piece of paper.

Several hours passed before I was finally able to pull it out. It was indeed from Ferko and contained a short message. He wrote *If I don't succeed in persuading your father to let me marry you, I will wait for you to come back to me. Here is my phone number. Don't lose it. I will love you forever. Your Ferko. 36-7853-0172*

"You know it by heart even after all these years?" Carmela raised her eyebrows. "Wow—you really loved him, didn't you?"

Paula Jean nodded and looked down. "I still have that note," she confessed. "I've kept it hidden away for 50 years. He was my first love..." her voice broke again and she hesitated then continued, "and I have to confess to you, he was the love of my life."

The tears fell freely then. Not only Paula Jean's but Carmela's, Janet's and Cecilia's as well.

"What an amazing story," Cecilia said quietly. "How did you bear this heartache for all these years?"

All Janet could say was "Wow" as she gazed compassionately at Paula Jean. Carmela, for once, was speechless. She covered her face with her handkerchief.

"You're probably wondering about Jack," Paula Jean stated flatly. "He was a good man, a very good man, more than you know. Since I've gotten this far, I'd better tell you the rest of the story."

"You mean there's more?" Janet reacted.

"Oh yes, there's more."

"Can we make another round of cappuccinos before you continue?" Carmela stood up and asked. "Or maybe we need to open a bottle of wine."

"I vote for the wine," chirped Cecilia. "I second that," echoed Janet.

"Then wine it is," Paula Jean said as she made her way to the kitchen. "I'll be right back."

Carmela and Janet collected the cappuccino mugs, took them into the kitchen, rinsed them and placed them carefully in the dishwasher. Paula Jean emerged from her walk-in pantry with four crystal wine glasses and a bottle of *Zenato Amarone della Valpolicella*, a traditional red wine that goes deliciously with a cheese platter which Paula Jean brought to the table moments later. The woman was incredible when it came to entertaining. Janet was fond of saying "You can take the woman out of the South but you can't take the South out of the woman."

Wine was poured all around, glasses clinked together with a subdued but hearty "To Friendship" and the women settled back down to hear the rest of the story. Every eye was on Paula Jean as she picked up the narrative where she'd left off.

"I had memorized Ferko's address and I managed to send him a postcard from Venice. Of course by the time he received it, we were on our way back to the States. I had written down my home address and telephone number that last night we were together. I told him I was afraid my father would be totally opposed to a proposal of marriage. I wanted him to know how to get in touch with me."

With an impish grin on her face, Paula Jean looked around the circle and said, "After we were home, I went looking for the postman who used to deliver our mail and I told him I was expecting a very important letter from Budapest and would he please make sure that he gave it directly to me when it came? I didn't want my father to find the letter in the mailbox before I saw it. The postman smiled knowingly and promised he would keep an eye out for it. You could do things like that in those days," she grinned.

"So, did he write you?" Cecilia probed.

"Yes, he did, and I wrote back. By this time we'd been home from Europe for a little more than a month." She inhaled sharply and closed her eyes. Carmela glanced knowingly at the other two, anticipating what was surely coming next.

"My mother had not been feeling well since we returned from the trip," Paula Jean said, "and finally gave in to my father's insistence that she go to the doctor. A few days later we learned that she had a tumor in her stomach and within the week, she underwent surgery. They said at the time that the operation was successful but Mom was never quite the same after that. Somehow or other, it affected her mind. No one ever figured out why but she was not the same person when she came home from the hospital. My father didn't handle it very well. He just didn't know what to do so he spent more and more time at work, less and less time at home."

Janet looked at Carmela with a 'how-could-you-have-thought-it-was-something-else' kind of look although, truth be told, they had all been thinking the same thing and were equally surprised when Paula Jean began talking about her mother.

"I quit my college classes to care for my mother. It was the right thing to do, " Paula Jean stated matter-of-factly. "It was hard, very hard. It was like taking care of a stranger. and just when I thought things couldn't get worse, they did."

She swallowed hard.

"I was so busy taking care of my mother that I lost track of time. About three to four weeks after Mother had come home from the hospital, I woke up in the middle of the night with severe abdominal pains and soon realized that I was bleeding heavily. Suddenly I realized something. It had been too long. My God, was I pregnant? If so,why was I bleeding? What was this terrible pain? Just when a girl in trouble needs her mother..." Paula Jean's voice broke.

"I'll spare you the details and go straight to the bottom line. I had a miscarriage before I even realized I was pregnant. I was nearly three months along. It was Ferko's child, of course. I'd never been with anyone else. I didn't dare tell my father. I couldn't tell my mother. I never felt so alone in my entire life." She paused.

"And the guilt–it was overwhelming, absolutely overwhelming. When a letter came from Ferko a few days later, I cried my heart out. How could I tell him I lost his child? It was horrible, just horrible," she lamented as fifty years of a bottled up grief came rushing to the surface like an angry river overflowing its banks. Paula Jean dropped her head into her hands til she was nearly doubled over as gut wrenching sobs issued from deep within her. "All those years that Jack and I couldn't have children," she divulged between sobs, "I'd cry over my lost baby. I never told Jack–I couldn't. I was afraid...."

Carmela, Janet and Cecilia were frozen in their seats, stunned by the unexpected revelations.

Carmela moved first. She slid off her chair, opposite the sofa and inched over on her knees to Paula Jean. Wrapping her arms around her friend, she wisely said nothing. She just cried with her. Janet and Cecilia took up their positions on either side of Paula Jean, surrounding her with the love, the understanding and the support she had needed fifty years before.

Time stood still. Nothing mattered but their friend.

Tissues piled up at Paula Jean's feet for several minutes until Carmela said softly, "Paula Jean, I'm so sorry you carried this pain alone for all these years. But guess what? It's out now and you're not alone anymore." With that, Carmela flung her arms open wide and exclaimed with exuberance, "We all need another glass of wine to celebrate!"

The other three looked at her completely perplexed, eyebrows raised. What in the world was she thinking?

"I read something one time, a quote that said something like "Real friendship happens when one person says to another: "What! You too? I thought I was the only one," proclaimed Carmela with gusto. "Don't you see what's just happened here? This is real friendship! We're much more than card-playing, pasta-loving, pearl-wearing friends! "

"And when did you become such a philosopher?" Janet inquired. "and by the way, you just stole a line from C.S. Lewis–well, sort of. He said it this way: Friendship is born **at the moment** when one person says to another: What! You, too? I thought I was the only one."

"Close enough," Carmela retorted. "The idea stayed in my brain because I liked it, even if I didn't remember it exactly." She paused and then in a somber tone unusual for Carmela, she continued, "There isn't a one of us who doesn't have pain or grief living somewhere in our memories. When someone chooses to finally talk about it, it's a very big deal. I really respect you, Paula Jean and I love you even more, my friend. Thank you–thank you for trusting us with your secret."

"Um, can I ask a question?" interjected Cecilia in her reserved and quiet way. "What prompted all of this? Is this connected to why you were so upset when we arrived."

Paula Jean rubbed her hands together nervously. She raised her eyes to the ceiling and took a deep breath.

"Ferko came to my door this morning."

The three of them stared with wide eyes and mouths hanging open. Carmela was the first to get hold of herself. "What?!?!" she shrieked. "Ferko–here–what the..." Janet and Cecilia slid forward and were on the edge of their seats.

Paula Jean raised her hands as if to say, 'Hold on; calm down.'

"I don't really know myself how he found me. We didn't get that far. I just wanted him gone before any of you arrived."

They all started talking at once. Paula Jean raised her hands again and the noise died away.

"Hold on, hold on," her voice steadier and stronger. "Let me finish. Ferko rang my doorbell earlier and I thought it was one of you arriving very early. Instead, I was shocked to see Ferko standing there. It's been fifty years but I recognized him instantly."

All at the same time, Janet, Cecilia and Carmela burst out with a string of questions, each one talking over the other one.

"What did he say? What did you do? Why did he come? How did he find you?"

"One at a time," Paula Jean responded. "I'm not sure I even remember everything he said but there was something about when he found out where I was, he came right away, and that he never forgot. He asked me if I ever forgot. He wants to take me out to dinner. Oh, I don't know what else. I was in shock, for heaven's sake!"

"Oh my," Cecilia said softly. She turned away from Paula Jean and stared out the window.

"Actually," Janet suggested philosophically, "it's probably the best thing that could have happened. What else would have ever brought you to the point of finally getting all that pain and fear out in the open? Now you can truly heal, my friend." Janet leaned over and gave Paula Jean a big hug, which was warmly reciprocated.

They talked on for awhile and a bit later, the wine glasses were re-filled and raised in a toast to true friendship. By the end of the afternoon, each of them expressed a sense of gratitude to Ferko, just for showing up. Carmela laughed and said, "It took a long lost Hungarian to get us to really open up. Good for him! Maybe that's enough reason for you to go ahead and finally marry the man."

The look of horror on Paula Jean's face made the other three convulse in gales of laughter. When they'd all caught their breath again, Janet called on her best managerial tone of voice and 'pontificated', as the others would say.

"Seriously, Paula Jean, why not? You love the guy. That's obvious. He loves you. That's obvious, too, or he wouldn't have come looking for you after all these years.

Why shouldn't you have some years of happiness with him after all this time?"

Paula Jean just shook her head and chuckled. "Seriously?" she replied. "Seriously,

a few hours ago I was making fancy sandwiches for my friends and now you want to marry me off so fast. Puhleeeeeese!" she ended with the strongest southern twang she could pull off.

The sound of laughter echoed through Paula Jean's house for several hours until the coming of dusk called each one back to their own home. As Paula Jean climbed into bed after one of the most traumatic days of her life, she was thankful for a new sense of light-hearted peace within herself. She was even more thankful for her friends–kindred souls she'd had the good fortune to discover in the countryside of Italy.

"Marry him?" she mused. "Hm, I can't believe she said that." She rolled over, turned off the bedside lamp and mumbled to herself, "A bride at 71? No way."

Chapter 6
Love and Loss

The chair was beautiful. Paula Jean surveyed the finished piece with a big smile and hugged Carmela warmly. "Thank you," she said, "as she dropped her purse on the sofa before circling the chair which had been transformed by the capable hands of Carmela.

Once a faded and stained navy blue, the wing chair was now a masterpiece in purple paisley with white cord trim. It was destined for Paula Jean's sitting room which she dubbed 'my purple retreat.' The smallest room in her home, it was nevertheless her favorite. It was in her purple retreat that she read, relaxed, wrote letters, said her prayers and crocheted exquisite scarves and other gifts for her friends.

These days it was also where she struggled with what she called the "Ferko issue".

Three weeks had passed since his startling appearance at her door. They had been out to dinner together twice and Ferko was pressing for another date. Paula Jean was reticent. Her inner turmoil was exceeded only by the enormity of the guilt and regret that had lingered in the recesses of her mind those nearly fifty years.

Carmela, Janet and Cecilia wisely held back, respecting their friend's need for the privacy that would lead to clarity. Their weekly lunches continued without interruption but the "Ferko issue" was studiously avoided. They had vowed that only Paula Jean had a right to bring him up and they would give her the latitude to decide when that would be.

But that didn't mean they weren't dying of curiosity! The phone lines sizzled from house to house with many a discussion between Carmela and Janet, or Janet and Cecilia or Carmela and Cecilia. They even tried a three way call once but Cecilia couldn't get her phone to cooperate. Janet insisted that the phone wasn't the problem, but that Cecilia was just 'technologically challenged'.

Carmela thought Paula Jean and Ferko should get married and enjoy however many years life would give them. Janet couldn't make up her mind how she felt about it and Cecilia, in true British fashion, called Carmela's proposal 'just so much rubbish.'

"But why?" Carmela asked during one of their lively discussions.

Clearing her throat, Cecilia sat up a little straighter and tilted her head towards Carmela. "They're a bit old, really," she began, her British lilt accenting the word, 'really'. Carmela rolled her eyes.

Ignoring the reaction, Cecilia defended her opinion. "Fifty years is a very long time," she declared. "People change. She has no idea what he's been through in those years. Good gracious, they hardly knew each other back then, let alone fifty years later. He doesn't really know her either. You don't just pick up where you left off after such a long time."

"She's got a point," Janet interjected, tilting her head towards Cecilia.

"Aw, you two are just so logical. Where's your spirit of adventure? Where's your romantic side?" Carmela quipped.

"I'll tell you where," Cecilia reacted. "I'm all for adventure but getting married at our age could easily become a nightmare rather than an adventure! Think about it! What if Ferko became ill, or suffered a stroke, or a heart attack, or something worse? Paula Jean doesn't need to end up being a debilitated old man's private nurse. She has a lovely life now. Why botch it up?" Cecilia declared emphatically. Then, wetting her lips she added, "Besides, I bet he has hair in his ears at his age. Ugh! Definitely not romantic."

Carmela burst out laughing while Janet raised her eyebrows nearly to her hairline and exclaimed, "Cecilia!! What a thing to say!"

"Well, you do have to think of those things, you know," Cecilia retorted defensively. Before Carmela had time to reply, Janet quickly changed the subject.

The next day all four of them met at Café Toscana for their favorite Cappuccinos before taking in a movie at the Odeon Cinema, the primary film theater in Florence for English speakers. It was a favorite of Janet's son and daughter-in-law and was the first place they had taken Janet after her move to Italy.

Being a movie lover, Janet had promptly told the others about the theater and soon it became a regular outing. Once a month or so, depending on what film might be playing at the theater, Carmela, Paula Jean, Cecilia and Janet met at the Café before going on to an afternoon matinee which usually began about 4 pm.

Quite often there would be considerable discussion regarding the choice of movie. Each of the women had a very definite opinion about what she liked–and disliked–and no hesitation whatsoever to make that opinion known. No quibbling this time. Their unanimous choice was the film 'RED' because all of them shared a common affection for the leading lady of the film, Helen Mirren. Cecilia, of course, was quite familiar with the British actress but she was a new face to Carmela and to Paula Jean when the four of them had seen the award winning movie, 'THE QUEEN', several months before.

Carmela's background in theater and drama made her the group's undisputed authority on good acting and once she pronounced her admiration for Mirren, complete with a detailed analysis of why the latter's performance was so brilliant, Helen Mirren was their uncontested favorite actress.

It was nearly dark as they left the theater. Paula Jean was effusive in her remarks about the white evening gown worn by Helen Mirren in a major scene during the movie. Cecilia thought the dress was lovely but was appalled that Mirren lifted a machine gun and fired while looking so elegant. Cecilia also remarked that if she'd been in charge of costuming, the dress would have been blue to bring out the color of Helen Mirren's eyes. Janet disagreed and tried to convince Cecilia that there was a symbolic intent encoded in the white dress. Carmela was far less interested in the dress. She loved the action scenes and the film's ending which came as something of a surprise to her. They were so busy talking as they made their way down the street that none of them noticed the two men walking toward them until Cecilia bumped into the taller of the two.

"Oh my, pardon me, please. I'm so sorry," she said, obviously embarrassed.

'*No c'e noia,*' the man replied, with a wave of his arm and a nod of his head.

He smiled, tipped his hat and said, '*Signora*' and walked on.

The women's conversation resumed but Janet stopped twice to look back at the retreating men. Carmela noticed and asked, "What's the matter?"

"The other man, not the one Cecilia bumped into–he looks familiar. I think I've seen him before but I can't place him," Janet replied. She shrugged her shoulders. "Maybe he just reminds me of somebody."

Much later that evening, Carmela had just settled into bed and was about to turn off the light when her telephone rang. For a moment she considered ignoring it, then thought better of it, rolled over and picked up the receiver.

"Hello," she said wearily.

"Hey, it's me. I think I know who.... It can't be...." It was Janet.

"What? Who are you talking about?"

"The man....the one in the street..."

"Janet, it's 11:30 at night. Go to sleep. Can't this wait until morning?"

"OK–sorry I woke you up." She clicked off before Carmela could say anything else.

'Aw, shucks', Carmela thought to herself. 'That wasn't nice.'

She reached for the phone and dialed Janet's number. After nine rings, Carmela put the phone down. 'Strange,' she thought. 'She just called me.' She picked up the receiver again, dialed and waited. Twelve rings. No answer.

'Maybe she's taking a bath,' Carmela thought. She rolled over, promising herself that she'd call again first thing in the morning.

Chapter 7
Unlikely Meetings

Taylor Broderick was a character in every sense of the word. From the tender age of five, he'd been an ongoing headache to his parents. There were times that the elder Broderick wondered if they'd done the right thing by adopting this child but he didn't dare breathe a word of it to his wife. She loved the boy and though she worried about him constantly, he was nevertheless her dream come true. She stubbornly believed that he would 'turn out fine if we just give him time.' Her husband doubted that but kept his misgivings to himself.

Though originally from Wales, the previous generation of Brodericks had moved to the east coast of England in 1929. Times were difficult in Wales during the 1920's. Unemployment was rampant and steadily increased until 23% of the population was out of work by 1927. Many Welsh families migrated east to England or north to Scotland. Some crossed the sea to Ireland looking for a better life. The Brodericks settled in Clacton-on-Sea, largest town on the Tendring peninsula, in Essex. Four generations had lived by the sea in Wales. The tradition would not be broken.

By the time Taylor was in his early teens, he'd had more than one brush with the local police and being dispatched to the Headmaster's office for unacceptable behavior was at least a weekly event.

At considerable sacrifice, Taylor's parents had enrolled him in Westcliff High School for Boys in Essex. Founded in 1920, the school imparted an excellent educational experience to boys between the ages of eleven and eighteen. Four long-serving Headmasters had guided the school since its inception, and exemplified the school's motto, *Courage and Strength*. In addition to academic excellence, great attention was given to developing the students' moral character. Integrity, reliability, self-discipline, initiative, punctuality and personal tidiness were given high priority within the overall curriculum. The school prided itself on having a program that took into account the full range of a developing boy's needs—physical, social, spiritual, cultural and academic. Taylor's parents felt that this was exactly what he needed.

To their credit, Mr. and Mrs. Broderick were honest with the Headmaster during the preliminary interview. They did not hide the fact that their son was something of a rebel, given to pushing boundaries and less than a stellar student. They were equally forthright in voicing their expectation that a disciplined environment, such as that offered by Westcliff High School for Boys, would have a positive effect on Taylor. They were successfully convincing. Taylor was accepted as a student.

After several dozen near expulsions from Westcliff, Taylor seemed to finally settle down and his last two years at the school were gratifying to his parents as well as to the surprisingly patient Headmaster. Truth be told, Headmaster Walker-Jones had a secretly held affinity for Taylor. He saw himself in the boy, though no one at Westcliff had any idea what kind of rascal the dignified Ryan Walker-Jones had been some forty years before.

After graduating from Westcliff, Taylor had a short-lived brush with higher education, decided that university studies didn't suit his fancy and enlisted in Her Majesty's Royal Air Force. In the course of extensive physical fitness testing and medical examinations, Taylor was asked to produce comprehensive medical records, including those of his parents and grandparents.

Philip and Bronwyn Broderick could keep the secret no longer. Taylor had never been told about the adoption but they dared not attempt to deceive the Royal Air Force with medical records that did not truthfully represent Taylor's genetic heritage.

With great trepidation, Philip and Bronwyn explained the truth to their son. He was not born in Wales as his legal birth certificate indicated. His 'parents' had not given birth to him, though their names were listed on the document. The truth was, they told him, that 19 years earlier they had adopted him with the help of a close friend from Wales who had emigrated to Canada. She was employed as assistant director of an international adoption agency that placed infants and children in childless homes throughout the British Commonwealth and as their friend, had taken a personal interest in facilitating the adoption.

Taylor's birthplace was Canada, the city of Toronto to be exact. He had been brought to Wales at the age of 21 days and before his first birthday, had legally become Taylor Broderick, son of Philip and Bronwyn Broderick of Tenby, Wales. His original birth certificate was destroyed. The new one reflected only his acquired Welsh identity. The documents of adoption, locked away in a small vault in the Broderick's attic, saw the light of day for the first time in nearly two decades.

Taylor stared blankly at the yellowed adoption certificate. Some woman he never knew existed had given birth to him in a Toronto hospital and for an unknown reason had given him away. Well, he thought, at least she let me live, whoever she was. His birth mother's name did not appear on the certificate. Neither was there any mention of who the father might be. There was only one hint pointing in part to his original identity. The official record named a baby boy, Thomas Edwards, as becoming the legal son of Philip and Bronwyn Broderick whose name would henceforth be Taylor Sydney Broderick.

He shrugged his shoulders and handed the document to his mother who had been watching him anxiously. He seemed largely unaffected. Bronwyn sighed audibly.

"So, there aren't any medical records, are there?" he asked.

"Well, no, son, there aren't," Philip replied. "Will that be a problem?"

"Don't know. I guess we'll find out." With that, Taylor got up and walked out the front door of the house. Philip and Bronwyn looked at each other.

"That was easier than I expected," Bronwyn said.

"I told you not to worry," Philip responded. "He's a young man. I didn't expect it to affect him terribly. Women get much more emotional about these things, Bronwyn."

In the end it wasn't the lack of medical records that deprived Taylor of a career with the Royal Air Force. His psychological profile indicated he was unsuitable for military life and the interviewer handling his enlistment suggested that perhaps he might look into a business career. "Pays better than the military," he remarked, as he wished Taylor success.

Handsome and charming, Taylor quickly found employment at the Sandrock Hotel, a leading seaside resort. His outgoing personality and winning smile made him a natural at public relations. The owners and the hotel guests loved him. Young female visitors were routinely infatuated with the dashing bell boy who delivered their luggage to their rooms.

Having decided within the first six months that he enjoyed working in a hotel environment, Taylor applied and was hired by the elegant and prestigious Grosvenor House Hotel in London as Head Concierge. Attired in the trademark Grosvenor uniform, he was strikingly handsome and therefore easily noticed by anyone and everyone who entered or left the hotel.

In less than a year Taylor's popularity and outstanding work ethic came to the attention of the hotel managers and Taylor was offered a promotion. The management wanted someone with his kind of presence to oversee the Reception Desk staff. This he did with excellence for two years when yet another promotion came his way. By the time Taylor celebrated his thirtieth birthday, he had advanced up the administrative ladder and had achieved the position of Vice-President for Guest Services. A team of well over 200 employees of the hotel fell under his supervision. They loved him for he learned all of their names, treated them with respect and never forgot an employee's birthday.

Philip and Bronwyn were rightfully proud of their son's success. Joining him for High Tea at the Grosvenor to celebrate that thirtieth birthday, they good naturedly recalled his tumultuous youth and Bronwyn didn't miss the opportunity to remind Philip that she had always said Taylor would 'turn out fine if we just give him some time.'

The issue of his adoption had never again been mentioned, either by Taylor or his parents.

It was at that same birthday celebration, that Philip and Bronwyn met their future daughter-in-law, the beautiful Catherine Bolton. Tall and slender with flowing dark hair, she and Taylor were a striking couple and the Brodericks couldn't be happier with the match. Catherine was intelligent as well as lovely, a warm and caring person. She hailed from a well established Essex family and they were especially delighted that her maternal grandmother was originally from Cardiff, the Welsh capital.

She and Taylor had been introduced by a mutual friend. It had been love at first sight. Their wedding was held at the Sandrock, where Taylor began his hotel career. Headmaster Ryan Walker-Jones was an honored guest and pronounced a toast to the happy couple, but only after regaling the wedding guests with humorous recollections of Taylor's early escapades at Westcliff High School for Boys. "My Lady Catherine," Walker-Jones said with a flourish, "you have your hands full." Everyone laughed as Taylor blushed. With wine glass raised, Catherine called out, "I can handle him."

Seven years and three grandchildren later, Taylor surprised his parents one morning with the news that he, Catherine and the children were moving to Italy. His success in the Grosvenor had earned him a stellar reputation among hoteliers throughout Europe and he had been offered a position that was too good to turn down. The Grand Hotel Villa Medici in Florence had enticed him with a generous relocation package along with a significant salary increase. He was to be their new General Manager, second in authority to the owner himself.

The Grand Hotel Villa Medici was an historical luxury hotel built in 1700. It was one of Florence's finest and attracted high-end clientele. It was furnished with exquisite antiques and tapestries and the sweeping views from the extra wide windows only added to its charm. In the world of hotel management, becoming the General Manager of the Grand Hotel Villa Medici was a prize to be envied.

Taylor assumed his new position two weeks after his thirty-eighth birthday. While Catherine settled the family into their new home, a rambling Tuscan villa just outside Florence, Taylor poured his energies into learning everything he needed to know in order to successfully manage and expand the hotel. He was smart and had a faultless memory. In no time, he was thoroughly familiar with the inner workings of the historic establishment, knew every staff member by name and was developing a plan for enhancing the hotel's business image and widening its appeal across Europe and the world.

Two months after arriving in Florence, Taylor was invited to the annual Fundraising Dinner hosted by the American International League of Florence, a non-profit charitable organization. In fact, the invitation had come to the hotel owner who deferred to Taylor and suggested that he and Catherine attend.

"It's a good place to meet other business leaders in *Firenze*," the elderly owner said. "Besides, since my wife passed away, I don't like going to these things by myself."

Taylor happily accepted and called Catherine right away. She was delighted at the prospect along with being a bit nervous. "What if they all speak Italian?" she asked Taylor on the phone. "That could be scary."

"Don't worry, honey," came his quick reply. "Business people today have to know English if they're going to get anywhere. It will be fine, I'm sure."

The evening of the gala event, Taylor left his office early. On the way home, he had a sudden impulse to stop by one of the many florist shops in Florence to pick up some flowers as a surprise for Catherine. She had worked diligently and single handedly to make their villa a warm and inviting home. He'd been so preoccupied with the hotel he really hadn't been much help. She deserved some flowers, he mused to himself. It's the least he could do.

Catherine was ready when he arrived, stunning in a royal blue silk dress, silver heels and her trademark diamond stud earrings, a wedding gift from her parents. Her wavy dark hair fell loosely around her shoulders and the faintest of make up enhanced her natural beauty. She looked like an Italian princess, Taylor thought, as he kissed her and presented the bouquet of roses to her.

"What are these for?" she asked, surprised.

"Just because I have the best wife in the world—that's all!" Taylor kissed her again and then took the stairs two at a time up to their bedroom on the second floor. He was back downstairs in no time, handsome as ever in a charcoal grey pinstripe suit, crisp white shirt and royal blue tie that complimented Catherine's dress.

The dinner was held at one of the areas most sought after event venues, the Villa Daniella Fucini, a beautiful Medicean villa from the 16th century exquisitely located in a relaxing landscape amidst the Tuscan hills just a few kilometers outside of Florence. Elaborate signs led the way to the largest of the three special event halls where uniformed ushers welcomed the League guests and escorted them to their pre-assigned tables. Catherine breathed a sigh of relief when she and Taylor were introduced to a couple already seated at the same table. The Canadian accent was unmistakeable but for Catherine, the accent was irrelevant. They spoke English–that's what mattered.

Taylor and Tom quickly struck up a conversation–all business, of course. Catherine and Jennifer connected as wives, mothers, and expats. Both were delighted to learn that their children's ages were nearly the same, which meant new friends for Daniel, Jonathan and Casey, Catherine and Taylor's three children. Daniel was 9 going on 29, Catherine told Jennifer, who promptly replied that her 10 year old, Matthew, tried to act like he was 30! Jonathan was almost exactly the same age, 7, as David, Tom and Jennifer's second child. The two boys had been born just 4 days apart. Casey, Catherine and Taylor's only girl, was 5 and Jennifer's youngest was also a girl, Heidi who was 4 ½. Before the main course was even served, the two mothers were already arranging play dates for their children.

Tom and Jennifer Bradshaw had been living in Florence some ten years already and assured Taylor and Catherine that life in Florence was second to none. They exuded happiness and enthusiasm about the area and all it had to offer. With so much in common, the two couples bonded immediately and became fast friends very quickly.

About three weeks later, Catherine was sitting at Jennifer's kitchen island, having coffee with her new friend, when Jennifer casually mentioned that her children's grandmother was coming to spend the weekend.

"Oh, your mother lives here?" Catherine asked.

"No, I wish," Jennifer smiled. "It's Tom's mother. My Mom lives in Ontario. But I must say, Janet's a great mother-in-law and easy to have around. We convinced her to move here after we came. She was alone in western Canada and we have her only grandchildren. It wasn't hard to talk her into coming." Jennifer laughed. "Now our problem is getting ourselves booked into her calendar. She's built quite a life for herself here. She's doing something all the time."

"Really?" said Catherine. "What is she doing?"

"Well, don't ask me how but she discovered three other women about her age, all expats, all English speakers, all living fairly close to one another and the four of them are something else. One of them is actually Mexican, I think, but she speaks perfect English. They're like the Three Musketeers except there's four of them. Maybe the Four Musketeers?" Jennifer chuckled. "None of them knew each other before they moved to Tuscany and now they're inseparable. They meet for lunch at each other's homes once a week, they frequently meet for coffee at Café Toscana, they go to the movies, they play cards, they go shopping, and who knows what else. Last week, I teased my mother- in- law on the phone by asking her if she remembered she moved here because we were here?

"You'll have to meet them, Catherine. They're really delightful women and Tom is actually very happy that his Mom has such good friends. But, my goodness, they are hilarious! They've got the best sense of humor–all of them–and they keep busy. It's amazing. Actually, I've thought several times that I hope I'm as happy and active as they are when I'm their age."

"Isn't that the truth!" Catherine echoed.

"What about your family, Catherine? Where are they?" Jennifer asked.

"Well, my Dad passed away about 3 years ago. I miss him a lot. We were very close. My Mom is still in our family home. I think I've convinced her to come visit us soon. She doesn't like to travel alone.

"Taylor's parents live in Essex in a small town by the sea northeast of London. They miss us and I know they want to come visit. They especially miss the grandchildren. They used to come to London at least twice a month. My father- in- law has Parkinsons. It's not really bad yet but I think he's hesitant to travel. Mom Broderick is working on him–convincing him to come. I think they will but it may be a few months down the road."

Catherine sighed. "It's bloody well difficult when you're far from your family, isn't it? If it weren't for that, Florence is a bit of paradise. I just love it here, all the color, the scenery, the food. I must admit I never tasted pasta in England as good as the pasta here. And I can't wait to see the poppy fields in full bloom. I hear it's a magnificent sight."

Jennifer nodded her head in agreement, "There isn't a picture in the world that does it true justice. I want to be with you when you first see them,"

"And the children are so happy," continued Catherine. "So is Taylor. He's loving his job."

Catherine glanced at the wrought iron clock on the wall. "I really must be going, Jen,"she said. "This has been great. Thanks for having me over." She gave Jennifer a quick hug and then giggled and said, "Hey, maybe we should start our own lunch-once-a-week tradition, just like your mother-in-law's friends. What do you think?"

"Great idea, Catherine," Jennifer responded enthusiastically.

"Next week, my house."

"You got it, girl friend." Jennifer called after her.

Catherine was already getting in her car. "See you then," she called back.

Chapter 8
The Man in the Street

Carmela poured herself a second cup of coffee and reached for the phone. She had dialed Janet's number more than once already but there was no answer. She counted off the rings as she walked over to the small table in her breakfast nook. She was about to hang up when Janet finally answered.

"Hello," said the familiar voice.

"Janet, it's me, Carmela. I've been so worried. Are you all right? I called you right back last night and you didn't answer and I've called already three times this morning. Where have you been?" Carmela blurted out.

"Oh, I'm sorry, Carmela," Janet responded in an apologetic tone. "I'm fine. I've been up in the attic looking for something and I guess I didn't hear the phone."

"Listen," Carmela continued, "I'm really sorry for being short with you last night. It wasn't very nice of me and that's why I called back. Can you forgive me?"

"My gracious, of course, Carmela. Don't give it another thought. It was silly of me to call, especially since it was so late."

"You seemed upset. Is everything OK?" Carmela pressed her.

"Everything's fine. It was the man in the street last night, remember? Cecilia bumped into one of them, but the other one–the young one–I don't know, Carmela. He just looked so familiar to me and after I got home, I had this strange thought that I might know who he is."

"OK," Carmela answered slowly, sensing something in Janet's voice.

"It's probably nothing and I'm just getting carried away." Janet seemed to want to change the subject.

Carmela, ever sensitive to other people's vibes, said brightly, "Hey, I'm going shopping today to look for a couple of gifts for my granddaughters. Want to come?"

"How soon are you leaving?" Janet asked.

"I could pick you up in about an hour. Would that work?"

"That's great. See you then."

"Hey, how about we go to The Mall?" Carmela suggested. She knew it was Janet's favorite shopping haunt.

"Now you're talking," Janet answered with a giggle.

As soon as she hung up the phone, Janet returned to the open box sitting in the middle of her living room floor. Though it was a bit heavy, the night before she'd managed to pull it out from under some other boxes stored in the attic and carried it down the narrow stairs and into the kitchen. Since it was after midnight, she made herself leave it there and went off to bed.

She was awake at six in the morning, threw on her robe and made her way to the kitchen. While the coffee maker did its duty, she carried the box into the living room and cleared the coffee table. She opened the box and started carefully lifting out old files and large overstuffed manila envelopes which she spread across the floor. As soon as the box was emptied, Janet went back to the kitchen to get her coffee, then padded back into the living room and sat on the floor. The search was on.

She looked in file after file, stopping occasionally to re-read an old newspaper clipping or pore over certain documents related to events in her life in days gone by. She didn't linger long with her memories. She was looking for something specific.

The phone rang twice, several rings each time, but she was so taken up with her search, she didn't even hear it. She had always been the kind of person who could get so deeply absorbed in a book that she would become oblivious to anything going on around her. That same intense focus on the task at hand was ruling her now.

Draining her coffee mug, Janet leaned back against the sofa and took a deep breath.

'*Where is it?*' she thought to herself. '*It has to be here somewhere.*'

Rolling over on one knee, she pulled herself up and went back to the kitchen for a second cup of coffee. Stiff from sitting on the floor, she took a few moments to stretch, berating herself for being out of shape. In her late 60's, Janet was actually in quite good shape by most people's standards, but not by hers. Cecilia used to tease her that she was "in denial" about her age. Janet always insisted that every woman should be able to touch her toes, even if she was 90.

The phone rang again and this time she answered. Finishing her conversation with Carmela, Janet knew she had an hour to herself. She could be ready in 20 minutes so settling back down on the floor again, she pulled a stack of manila envelopes closer. Picking up the first one, she happened to glance at the one below it and three words written with a red felt tip pen caught her eye: JULIE'S MEDICAL RECORDS.

Casting the first envelope aside, she grabbed the second one and started pulling pages out of it. Some of them were stapled together while others were loose and frayed on the edges. She thumbed through each page, looking, looking.

Finally she found it. She bit her lip as her eyes scanned the page. After reading to the bottom line, she closed her eyes and sighed heavily. Images flooded back into her mind of that horribly painful day nearly 40 years earlier. She let them flow through her like a motion picture demanding its own re-run.

'She was so young,' Janet thought. 'So many years and I still miss her.' She wiped a lone tear from her cheek and sighed. She returned the stack of manila envelopes to the empty box then glanced at the clock. Carmela would be arriving in half an hour. The rest of the files and envelopes would have to wait on the floor until she returned from the trip to The Mall.

Short on time, Janet pulled her favorite charcoal grey slacks from the closet and chose a pearl grey cashmere sweater to go with them. She was showered and dressed in 10 minutes, applied minimal make-up and pulled her hair back with a black velvet ribbon. She had just finished emptying the grounds from the coffee maker and washing her mug when she heard the familiar toot of Carmela's car.

Glancing at the array of files and papers on the living room floor, Janet coded the alarm, then went out the door and down the stairs to join Carmela.

It was a beautiful Tuscany day. Bright sunshine took the edge off the chill in the air. They drove the few miles into town chatting about inconsequential things like the latest recipe Carmela had tried and the book Janet was presently reading–nothing personal, nothing emotional. Janet thought again how grateful she was for Carmela's friendship and for who Carmela was as a person. They were very close, the best of friends, yet she could always count on Carmela to respect her privacy. Carmela always gave people the right to talk when they wanted to and she was a terrific listener. But she also gave her friends the right to keep to themselves when they needed to and never engaged in trying to coax anyone to confide in her. She had the kind of moral character that made her a superb friend. *No wonder we all love her*, Janet mused to herself, glancing over at Carmela, humming as she drove down the roadway.

About thirty minutes drive south of Florence on the A-1 there is a shopping mall in the beautiful hills of Tuscany, simply known as **"The Mall"**. The drive alone is worth the trip. Golden fields dotted with centuries old stone castles follow each other like a living art gallery. "It's truly like driving through a picture postcard," Carmela remarked as they sped along.

The Mall itself is a rather modern building situated in a park like setting. The women like the fact that the parking is free and plentiful; there is an ATM machine and, of course, a typical Tuscan style café. It was Janet and Carmela's first stop.

They chose a table by the window of the café perfectly situated for one of their favorite pastimes: people watching. Ordering two cappuccinos and one large almond croissant to share, they settled back in the comfortable chairs as a tall, rather portly blond woman passed by the window. She was dressed in a bright yellow pants suit, royal blue heels and an orange wide brim felt hat. She carried an oversize royal blue leather purse that sported yellow and orange stripes down its center.

"Wow! Did you see that?" Carmela raised her left eyebrow. "Looks like Big Bird...or his Aunt Sophie!"

"Didn't know Big Bird had an Aunt Sophie" Janet responded, as she and Carmela stifled their giggling. "She kind of screams 'American tourist', doesn't she?"

"I suppose," Carmela replied. "or maybe she's just screaming 'Look at me'. Don't you sometimes wonder what goes through people's minds when they dress like that?"

The two friends lingered for the next half hour over the croissant and the coffee, making small talk and watching for more interesting people to walk by. Then they paid the bill and sauntered out into the mall.

Strolling through this particular mall was like thumbing through a Vogue magazine. Name brand shops were everywhere: Gucci, Yves Saint Laurent, Stella McCarthy, Burberry, Armani, and the like, as well as a few local retailers whose merchandise was of equal quality and sported a local high-end label of one or other Tuscan designer. The window displays were beautifully appointed and smiling salespeople greeted the potential shoppers at the entrance of each shop. Fortunately, the prices were as impressive as the fashion. Most items were roughly fifty to seventy percent lower than retail and if you walked to the back of many of the stores you often found items that were reduced even further.

That was Carmela's favorite place—the back of the store. She was a bargain hunter from way back and was heard to say frequently that the only way to raise six children and have them well dressed was to develop the art of finding bargains. She had definitely mastered the art.

Janet on the other hand had an eye for quality and loved well-made sensible clothes that were also fashionable and durable. She preferred finding what she liked, paying whatever it cost and then wearing it for several years, varying the accessories as needed. She didn't have the patience to bargain hunt like Carmela did. Their different styles of shopping had been the subject of more than one lively discussion.

This day Carmela was on the hunt for children's clothes. Her twin granddaughters would be turning 8 in two weeks and she wanted to send them Italian made dresses, the kind with the exquisite embroidery typical of the region. The twins were identical in appearance and mannerisms and their mother enjoyed dressing them alike most of the time. They were so much alike that at times even Carmela's daughter-in-law, the twins' mother, wasn't sure which one she was talking to. The girls, Mindy and Mandy, loved it–and pulled their share of identity pranks.

About an hour into the search, Carmela happened upon a lovely raspberry colored dress in the right size and at the right price, but there was only one. Seeking out a sales woman, she explained that she had twin granddaughters and therefore needed two of the same dress. Was there another one?

The clerk was doubtful but hurried away to ask the department manager. A few moments later, the manager returned with regrets that the raspberry colored dress was the last of its kind but she carried in her hand two identical dresses very similar in style to the first one. They were a lovely shade of aqua and beautifully embroidered but the price was a good bit higher than the original dress Carmela had chosen.

Not to be deterred, Carmela launched into negotiations. Within five minutes, she and Janet were out the door, the aqua dresses purchased at the lower price and beautifully gift-wrapped besides at no extra charge. The department manager was seen shaking her head, though smiling, as the two women left the store. She turned to the clerk who had first waited on Carmela and said "She was so nice about it–what else could I do?" The young clerk just smiled.

"I don't know how you do that," Janet said as they walked back toward the entrance of The Mall. "I'd never have the nerve to ask the manager to give me the new season's merchandise at the sale price of last season's clearance dresses."

"Stick with me, girlfriend," Carmela winked. "I'll save you money every time."

Getting back into the car, Carmela popped one of her favorite CD's into the stereo system, a collection of classic masterpieces, then turned the key to start the engine. They pulled out of the massive parking lot and turned left towards the A1 for the drive home. The afternoon sun was hanging low in the western sky, turning the fields even more golden than their normal daytime hue. Janet was exceptionally quiet for most of the trip. Carmela stole a glance or two along the way but Janet was in her own world, mostly staring out the front window but twice turning her head to the side as they passed some of the more opulent castles.

"Penny for your thoughts," Carmela said quietly, as they were nearing the end of their drive.

"Sorry," Janet turned quickly toward Carmela. "I'm sorry," she repeated. "I guess I haven't been much company, have I?"

"Something bothering you?" Carmela asked.

"Sort of," Janet hesitated and looked out the window again. Then suddenly she turned toward Carmela, "Do you need to go right home?" she asked.

"No," Carmela looked over at Janet. "Why?"

"Oh, I don't know. Maybe this is just silly and I shouldn't bother you with it."

"What?" asked Carmela, as they pulled up in front of Janet's home.

"Do you have time to come in for a bit?" Janet asked.

"Thought you'd never ask," smiled Carmela, unbuckling her seat belt and opening her door.

Walking through Janet's front door, Carmela was surprised to see the piles of manila envelopes, papers and file folders in disarray across the living room.

"Here," Janet indicated a spot on the sofa as she moved a stack of file folders onto the floor. "Have a seat. I'll put some water on for tea." She disappeared into the kitchen, leaving Carmela to survey the mess that surrounded her.

I wonder what this is about, Carmela thought to herself.

She didn't have long to wait. Janet was back in no time bearing a tray with two cups of tea and a plate of her homemade gluten free peanut butter cookies, a favorite of the foursome. She set the tray down on the ottoman since the coffee table was covered with papers. Handing one cup to Carmela, she picked up the other one for herself and with her free hand, perched the plate of cookies on top of a stack of files in the middle of the coffee table.

"Cecilia and Paula Jean would never believe this, you know," Carmela teased. "Janet Bradshaw serving tea in the middle of a messy living room–and balancing a plate of cookies on top of a pile of papers? Oh, can you imagine what the Brit and the Southern lady would say?" Carmela laughed heartily and Janet joined in.

"It *is* pretty funny, isn't it? So unlike me," Janet acknowledged.

"So what *is* all this mess?" Carmela ventured to ask.

Janet half-smiled and said, "It all started with Cecilia bumping into that man. I don't think I would have even noticed them otherwise."

"Noticed what?" Carmela inquired.

Janet leaned over and picked up a manila envelope. Carmela noticed the bright red letters on the front of it and almost asked, "Who's Julie?", but decided to hold her tongue. *Let Janet take the lead*, she told herself.

Pulling a sheaf of documents from the envelope, Janet flipped through them until she found one that had a passport size photo of a young girl. The family resemblance was obvious and for a moment, Carmela wondered if it was an old picture of Janet herself.

Gesturing toward the photo, Janet said quietly, "This is my sister, Julie. She was younger than me by four years and my only sibling. Actually, my mother did have a baby boy between me and Julie but he was stillborn. Even though I never saw him, he was still sort of real to me because my Mom always lit a candle on his birthday." Janet paused. "I don't think Mother ever really got over the loss of that baby boy."

"Anyway," she continued, "back to my sister. Julie was a good girl, did well in school and she used to want to follow me everywhere. Of course, you know what that's like when you're 18 and your sister is 14. You don't want her around all the time!" Janet shook her head, her lips forming a sad half-smile. "Since we were about the same size, she helped herself to my clothes too often for my liking, especially since she did so without asking. I remember one time in particular. I came home to get ready for a date and the dress I had planned to wear was nowhere to be found. I was SO annoyed! Sure enough, Julie had worn it to school that day–to school, mind you!! It was crumpled up in the laundry basket, covered with chocolate stains. I was furious!"

Carmela smiled. "I know all about that. Remember, I had eight sisters."

"Wow, I don't know how you survived that," Janet remarked.

"Wouldn't trade it for the world," was all Carmela would say.

"I keep digressing. Sorry–I hope I'm not boring you with my memories."

"Not at all, Janet," Carmela squeezed Janet's hand. "Tell me more."

"Julie was sixteen when Carl and I were married. We moved from our home town of Hamilton–that's near Toronto–to the big city of Edmonton in western Canada. Carl had just graduated from university and landed a great position." Janet laughed. "You should have seen our first apartment. It was tiny–the kitchen was like a closet. There was one bedroom and after we put a double bed in there, we could just barely walk around it to get into the bed. The living room was about the size of my present bathroom!" she exclaimed. "And you know what? We thought we were living the high life. We had our own place. That was a big deal back then. When I think of it now, I have to laugh. But we were happy."

"Reminds me of the first place Pedro and I had in Mexico. It was just one big room that served as kitchen, living room, and bedroom with a bathroom out the back door of the house, built against the outside wall. At least we had running water–even hot water," Carmela chuckled. "We were happy, too."

"Julie started dating soon after we were married and my mother would call me frequently saying she was worried about my sister. She felt that Julie wasn't always choosing the best boys to go out with and Mom was concerned. She asked me to talk to Julie which I did but I don't think it made much of a difference.

"In all fairness to Julie, I think Mom was a bit over-protective. In the summer we went back to Toronto to visit the family and I met one or two of the boys that Julie went out with. They seemed nice enough to me. Carl agreed. He also thought Mom was overly worried without reason.

"At any rate, when I was pregnant with Tom three years later, Julie called me one day to announce that she was engaged. She was very excited and wanted to bring her fiance to Edmonton to meet us. They arranged to come on the bus the following week. Julie was about to turn nineteen at the time and Brian, her intended, was twenty-one.

"Carl and I were positively impressed with Brian. He seemed very responsible and mature for his age. He was the eldest of seven children and had held a job since he was fourteen. When he proposed to Julie, he was a carpenter's apprentice and earning a reasonably good salary for his age. They were obviously very much in love and we gave them our blessing. Mom and Daddy did as well. In fact, my father was quite happy that Julie was marrying Brian. He told me he was comfortable putting his 'baby girl' into Brian's care. What I didn't know then was that my Dad had been diagnosed with cancer. He didn't tell anyone, not even my Mom, until after Julie's wedding.

"Do you want more tea, Carmela?" Janet interrupted her narrative. "Yours must be cold."

"No, no, it's fine," Carmela glanced at the nearly full cup. "I'm so caught up in your story that I forgot all about the tea. Don't worry about it–please, go ahead."

Janet leaned over and picked up the stack of papers she had earlier taken out of the manila envelope. She leafed through them and pulled out a yellowed document that had KENSINGTON MEMORIAL HOSPITAL across the top in bold black letters. She laid it on her lap.

After a few moments punctuated by a heavy sigh, Janet continued.

"Julie got pregnant about a year later. While my pregnancy with Tom was a breeze, hers was just the opposite. She had a very hard time. Morning sickness was all-day sickness for her. She lost a great deal of weight, so much so that by the fourth month she was hospitalized and they were feeding her with a tube for about 10 days. We were all pretty worried, most of all Brian. The doctors kept assuring him that the baby was growing normally and that Julie's condition would pass. Julie came home but a month later was back in the hospital. She just couldn't keep anything down and was getting weaker all the time. For the next four months, Julie was on complete bed rest in the hospital. It was really tough, especially on Brian. But it was pretty tough for me, too. Here I was, so far away, while my baby sister was having such a hard time."

"How far is it actually?" Carmela asked. "I've never been to Canada."

"Minimum three days driving–and that's minimum," Janet answered. "And we didn't have a car in those days. We had to take the train so it was even longer."

"That must have been very hard for you," Carmela said sympathetically.

Janet nodded and continued.

"A month before the due date, Julie went into labor. They tried to stop it but they couldn't. The baby was in distress and Julie was extremely weak. They delivered by Ceasarian–a little boy, 4 lbs 14 ozs at birth. They told us that though he was tiny, he was breathing normally and would be just fine. Somehow despite his mother's difficult pregnancy, he was a strong little guy. He was in the neonatal intensive care unit at first and we thought he'd be there quite awhile but he surprised us all. He gained weight much more quickly than the pediatrician anticipated and at eight days had topped 5 lbs., the minimum weight he needed to be in order to leave the hospital. We were overjoyed when Mom called to say that the baby would be leaving the hospital two days later. Julie was still pretty weak but the doctor felt she'd made enough of a recovery to return home, provided Mom would care for the baby and give Julie time to complete her recovery. Of course, Mom was more than happy to do so. Julie would live at Mom and Dad's, back in her old bedroom, for as long as it took for her to regain her strength. By then we all knew that Dad was fighting cancer and we hoped that a new baby in the house would be a positive uplift for him. Besides he seemed to be holding his own at the time. Carl and I planned to make the trip to Hamilton a few days later to see our new nephew.

"Early the next morning–about 5 am–the phone rang. It was Mom and she was sobbing. I couldn't understand her because she was crying so hard. Dad took the phone and in the saddest voice I ever heard from my father said simply, "Janet, you need to come home. It's Julie. She's...she's gone." He broke down crying. I think I went into shock. I just stared at Carl who grabbed the phone from my hand and shouted into it, "What happened?"

By then Dad had composed himself somewhat. He told Carl that Julie had started hemorraghing around midnight. When they couldn't stop the bleeding, the doctor called Brian, who rushed to the hospital. He was by her side when Julie passed away about 3 am.

Brian was distraught. I'm sure he was also in shock. He couldn't even call Mom and Dad. The doctor did it for him and broke the news to my parents.

Janet sighed deeply then turned to Carmela.

"I'm sorry. I've probably given you way more details than you needed to hear. This was an awfully long story but it is leading up to something. I'll cut this short and just get to the end of the story.

"Carl and I made the long trip for Julie's funeral. Tom was nearly two and a half then and we hoped that his presence would be something of a comfort to my parents. It was so hard, Carmela. Mile after mile on that long trip, I kept trying to grasp the reality that my baby sister was gone. She wasn't going to be there when I arrived.

What could I possibly say to Brian? And what about my new little nephew? That tiny, precious life robbed of his mother ...it was just awful. I had no idea the situation was going to get even worse."

Janet wiped away a tear. Carmela just looked at Janet with wide eyes.

"When we finally arrived in Hamilton, Dad was waiting for us at the station. I hadn't seen him in a few months and I was shocked. He'd lost a great deal of weight and looked gaunt. He was very pale and most of his hair was gone because of chemo. His eyes were sunken in and honestly, all I could do was hug him and cry. He probably thought I was crying for Julie–and I was–but I was also crying for him. I just wanted to hold on to him and never let go.

"Dad was pretty quiet on the short ride to the house. He hugged Tommy a lot when we first arrived and kept asking me if I was OK. "As OK as I can be under the circumstances, Dad," was all I could say.

"I couldn't wait to get to the house to see Mom and the new baby. I had imagined myself picking him up, holding him close to me and whispering in his ear that everything would be OK, that he still had a family that loved him and we'd take care of him. I had no idea what to say to Brian except to cry with him. There really isn't anything you can say at a time like that.

"Mom stood in the doorway as we pulled into the driveway. I remember thinking that she looked so old, so frail. I flew out of the car, bounded up the three steps to the porch and burst through the storm door into her arms. We cried and cried. Carl carried little Tommy in and took him straight up to bed. It was late and Tom had fallen asleep in the car.

"When I finally got a hold of myself, my first question to Mom was, 'Where's the baby?' I want to hold him."

She looked at Dad and then back at me. Tears poured down her face as she quietly said to me, "Honey, the baby's not here. He's in Toronto. Brian has decided to give him up for adoption."

"Carmela, I screamed. The first and last time in my life that I ever screamed but when my mother said those words, I screamed, 'NO–NO–NO' Carl came running down the stairs, jacket flying, his eyes wide with terror. He ran over to me and just held me while he looked at Mom and Dad. He told me later he didn't know what to think when he heard me scream like I did. Poor Carl. I scared the heck out of him.

"He can't do that!" I yelled. 'He can't do that. Why? Why? Mom, we've got to go and stop him. Get the baby back.' I just kept talking like that, like a crazed woman, looking from Carl to Mom to Dad.

"Carl finally calmed me down and walked me into the living room. Mom and Dad sat opposite me on the loveseat. Dad was holding Mom's hand and when I quieted enough to be able to hear him, he spoke. His voice was hoarse and fraught with emotion.

"Janet," my Dad said, "let me tell you what happened. Brian is in a bad way. He's destroyed, he's distraught at the loss of Julie. He's convinced that he can't be father and mother to this little one, that he's not in any condition to take that on and that he doesn't know when he'll ever be able to." Dad's voice broke and he stopped for a few moments and looked down at the floor.

Then turning toward me, he said, "I stood by his side at the hospital, honey, when he made the decision. He was holding the baby, just staring at him, and then he kissed the baby's forehead and turned toward me. . 'Dad,' he said, 'please don't hate me. Try to understand. I love this little boy with everything in me. He's the most beautiful thing Julie and I ever made. But he needs a good home; he needs a Mommy and a Daddy so he can grow up happy and healthy. I can't give that to him right now. I feel like a big part of me died when Julie died. Can you understand that? I can't ask you and Mom to raise him–that's not fair. It's not even reasonable. Janet and Carl are so far away. I can't expect them to just take on my son–just like that. So I have decided that the best thing I can do for this baby is let him be adopted by a good family. I really want to do what's best for him.' Then Brian kissed his son and handed him over to a nurse.

I was about to plead with him to wait, not to make a quick decision that he would regret later, but suddenly, he turned and said to me, 'Please help Mom and Janet and Carl understand'. Then Brian ran out of the hospital. We haven't seen him since."

"Carmela, it was the most awful day of my life. It was almost too much. I couldn't process it. I couldn't accept it. I wanted to raise my sister's boy if she couldn't. He was part of her. I could hold on to her through him. That's the way I felt. I cried my heart out in Carl's arms.

"Brian did show up the next morning. He came to the house a couple of hours before the funeral. By then I had done a lot of praying and thinking. Carl and I had talked late into the night. We both went straight to him when he arrived and we hugged him. We said nothing. We just hugged him and the three of us cried together.

After the funeral, Brian came to tell us he was leaving that afternoon for Vancouver where his grandmother lived. He said he needed to go spend some time with her. We had always known Brian adored his grandmother. He had spent a great deal of his childhood with her after his parents had divorced when he was seven. He never said why and we never asked him about his early years. We just figured if he wanted to talk about it he would.

"We tried to get him to stay and talk with us. We wanted to offer to take the baby, to raise him. But he hurried away." Janet paused as Carmela squeezed her hand.

"You know, we really loved Brian, Carmela. He was a very good husband to Julie. We just couldn't understand how he could give his son away."

The sun had long since set and by now it was dark. Janet glanced at the clock on her mantel and was shocked that it was nearly 7:30 pm.

"Oh my gosh, Carmela." Janet jumped up. "I had no idea it was so late. Are you hungry? What can I get for you? How about an omelet? I've got some spinach and cheese and...."

"Whoa," Carmela interrupted. "Hold on. You still haven't made the connection for me. What does all this have to do with your calling me at 11:30 last night?" Carmela tilted her head to one side and looked up at Janet with questioning eyes.

"Ah....." Janet plopped down on her knees in front of the sofa and rocked back on her ankles.

Hm, thought Carmela, *wish I was that flexible!*

"The man in the street last night. You're probably going to think I'm absolutely crazy but I'm going to say it anyway. The man walking up the street, not the one Cecilia bumped into, but the other one. Carmela, he is the spitting image of Brian.

What are the chances of that?"

Carmela raised both eyebrows and opened her mouth to say something but Janet jumped in first.

"I know–I know what you're going to say. I know–it's probably pretty far-fetched and you can say all that stuff about everybody in the world has a twin somewhere, blah, blah, blah. But Carmela, he didn't just look like Brian–I mean, if I didn't know better, I would think I was looking at Brian himself, the way he looked some thirty years ago! I'm serious!"

Chapter 9
Weekend

"Grandma!" squealed Heidi as she bounded across the floor and threw herself into Janet's open arms. Jennifer leaned over her daughter to welcome her mother-in-law with a kiss on the cheek.

"Grandma, Grandma, I can read now. Wanna hear me?" Heidi pulled her grandmother's arm toward the living room.

"Hold on, Heidi. Let Grandma take her coat off," Jennifer gently chided the four year old.

Janet pulled a small package from her purse and handed it to Heidi. "Here, sweetheart, why don't you see what this is," Janet smiled at her bright-eyed little granddaughter. Heidi grinned and then giggled as she pulled off the red ribbon and tore apart the striped paper in which the package was wrapped. Lifting out a delicate bracelet made of tiny pink glass beads, her eyes danced with delight. "Look, Mommy, look!" she exclaimed with obvious excitement.

"Oh, how pretty! And what do you say to Grandma?" Jennifer asked.

Heidi threw her arms up towards Janet. "Thank you, Grandma. It's so pretty." Janet reached down to hug the little girl as she winked at Jennifer. "Such a girly girl–I love it!" she remarked.

"How about some tea, Mom?" Jennifer asked as she hung Janet's coat up and picked up her overnight bag. "I'll put the water on and take your bag to your room." Tilting her head in Heidi's direction, she added, "A certain little girl has been running to the window every five minutes since I told her you were coming," Jennifer laughed. "She'll probably talk your ear off–at least until the boys get home from school."

Minutes later, Jennifer returned to the living room with a tray of freshly baked cookies and two mugs of mint tea, her mother-in-law's favorite, as well as a glass of milk for Heidi.

"I made the cookies today, Grandma," Heidi chirped. Then glancing at her mother, with a twinkle in her eye she said, "Mommy helped me, but just a little bit."

Jennifer rolled her eyes and grinned at Janet. "Oh, we think we are SO grown up!" she remarked to her mother-in-law. Janet made a big deal of taking the first bite and raving about how delicious the cookie was, delighting Heidi who clapped her hands and said, "Daddy says I'm a good cooker, just like Mommy."

Matthew and David came in from school about an hour later, proudly waving their report cards. "All A's, Mom," Matthew announced as he dropped his book bag in the middle of the kitchen.

"Hey, I said I was gonna show her my report card first," David interjected. "No fair," he scowled at his brother. "You do that all the time."

"Come here, boys," Janet jumped in. "Let me see those report cards." David thrust his into his grandmother's hand. "Great job, David," Janet remarked as her eyes scanned the card. "I'm really proud of you." She planted a loud kiss on the top of his head. "Where's yours, Matthew?"

Jennifer smiled and handed Matthew's report card across the kitchen island to Janet. Another row of A's and even an A+ in Math. "Wow–two boys in the same family with straight A's. We'll have to celebrate!" Janet remarked. The boys beamed.

"How about my two *brilliant* boys go upstairs and *brilliantly* clean up their room?" Jennifer gave her boys the kind of Mom smile that says I-love-you-now-go-do-what-I-said! They knew better than to say anything but 'yes, Ma'am'. She called after them as they started up the stairs, "There's fresh cookies waiting for you as soon as you're done."

"So what's new with the Four Musketeers?" Jennifer turned to Janet after the children had left the kitchen.

"Not much," Janet responded. "I went shopping with Carmela yesterday. She found the most adorable dresses for her twin granddaughters, and as usual, managed to get them at an amazing price. " Janet chuckled as she added, "You don't really go *shopping* with Carmela. You go on an *adventure*!"

"The way I see it," Jennifer answered, " you four women are one big adventure after another! You guys are amazing. I was just telling Catherine about you the other day and remarked that I hope I'm as active and vibrant as you all are when I'm your age."

"Who's Catherine?" Janet inquired.

"A new friend. She and her husband just moved here a couple months ago; really nice couple. Tom and I met them at a dinner we attended recently; you know, one of those functions that come with the job. It was actually a nice event. This new couple was seated at our table. They're from England. He's in the hotel business. They have three children almost the same age as ours which made for immediate conversation. I was so thrilled to find out about children the same age as ours. In fact, our kids have already met for a play date."

"That's great," Janet remarked. "For the kids and for you, too. Living in a foreign country, it's always nice to find some new friends that you can relate with. What does Catherine do?"

"I think she's a stay at home Mom. I don't know a lot about her yet. We saw each other at the park when the kids played together but didn't have much time to talk about personal things, just the usual two-Moms-at-the-park kind of talk. I did have her over a couple of days ago for coffee and our conversation was primarily about Florence and living here–stuff like that. I really like her, Mom; she seems to be a really nice person. I think we'll be good friends."

As an afterthought, Jennifer added, "I did tell her about you and your friends. She thought it was really cool. In fact, I think we're going to start meeting regularly for lunch like you guys do. But don't worry, Mom," Jennifer smiled broadly. "We won't crash your party at Café Toscana. We'll find someplace else to go."

Later that evening, after the children were asleep, Tom, Jennifer and Janet settled themselves comfortably in the living room with steaming mugs of hot chocolate, the favorite Bradshaw family beverage. With a flick of his wrist, Tom popped the footrest of the brown leather recliner and leaned back, stretching his long legs and emitting a long sigh. "Long day?" Janet inquired.

"Aren't they all?" he replied. "Good, though. Got a lot done today."

"Any news on that big contract?" Jennifer asked him.

"Still waiting," he answered. "Takes time when there's so much money involved."

Turning to his mother, he said, "We've got a proposal out to represent a major European hotel chain. I'm working on the deal so they'll be my client if it goes through. You know what that means."

Janet nodded. "Proud of you, son," she said simply. Tom smiled.

"How are all your buddies?" he asked, changing the subject. "The Tuscany Golden Girls," he snickered.

Janet laughed. "I won't tell them you said that. " She took another sip of her chocolate. "Everybody's fine. We went to see the movie *RED* the other day. We all really liked it. Have you seen it?"

"Can't say that I have? Who plays in it?" Tom asked.

"Helen Mirren, Morgan Freeman, Bruce Willis..."

"I like Freeman. He's a great actor," Tom commented. "And Helen Mirren was amazing in the *QUEEN*." Turning to Jennifer, he said, "I bet Taylor and Catherine like Mirren, being from England and all. Maybe we should do the double date thing one of these days and go to a movie with them," he said. "What do you think?"

"I'm always ready for a night out," Jennifer grinned at her husband. "Just tell me when."

"I'll babysit," Janet interjected with a grin.

"You're on, Mom," Tom replied. "Can't pass up a free baby sitter."

"Who said I'm free?" Janet retorted with a sly grin. "I have my price, you know."

Eyebrows raised, Tom looked questioningly at his mother.

"Jennifer's home made pizza with lots of garlic and onions–enough for me and the kids and an extra one to take home for my–for the Golden Girls!" she declared with a flourish.

"Deal!" Jennifer lifted her mug in a mock toast. "When can we go?" she turned toward her husband.

The weekend passed quickly as it always did when Janet visited with her family. The grandchildren loved having her there as did Tom and Jennifer. They never took for granted the warm relationship they had with Janet. For her part, Janet never regretted moving to Italy so she could be near her only son and his family. Jennifer was the daughter she'd never had and she treasured their open and loving connection. And having suffered through an overbearing mother-in-law in her early years, Janet had learned what *not* to do in a relationship with a daughter-in- law.

Carl's mother had been the epitome of the meddling mother-in-law and the source of tremendous stress in Janet and Carl's marriage. Truth be told, she was the major reason behind their move from Hamilton to Edmonton, not Carl's job. His mother never knew it but he'd been offered an equally good job in Toronto when he graduated from University. They'd been married eighteen months at that time and Janet had already had enough of Mother Bradshaw. The job offer in Edmonton was their ticket to freedom, Janet thought, and convinced Carl to take it.

They *were* happy in Edmonton, at least in the early years. But as time went on, Carl began making more and more solo visits to his mother in Toronto. At first he would go for a weekend here and there. When Janet wanted to go with him so she could see her family as well and take Tommy to see his grandparents, Carl used the excuse that they couldn't afford three train tickets. The first time the three of them actually made the trip together was when Julie died. Afterwards, Carl continued his solo trips to Toronto. Janet became suspicious that perhaps there was another woman.

When she confronted Carl, he was outraged, saying that he was helping his mother who was not well and needed him. The fact that his wife and young son also needed him seemed to escape him. In the end, there *was* another woman–but not the kind that Janet feared. The *other woman* was indeed his mother. Carl was a grown man on the outside but on the inside he was a little boy who couldn't leave 'Mommy'. Janet divorced him when Tom was eight.

The elder Mrs. Bradshaw blamed the divorce squarely on Janet and forbid her son from having anything to do with his ex-wife or his son. Spineless as he was, he did her bidding. Janet raised Tom on her own with no support of any kind from the boy's father. Tom bumped into his father once when he was a teenager during a visit that he and his mother made to Hamilton to see her family. That was over twenty years earlier. Neither Janet nor Tom had heard anything from Carl since.

Janet lay in bed awake that night and thought of Carl. She was no longer angry or hurt. She had left that behind many years before. She thought about the wonderful weekend she'd had with Tom and Jennifer and her beloved grandchildren and she surprised herself at feeling a sense of pity arise within her for the first time. She realized that she couldn't even recall the pain of betrayal she had felt in the distant past.

It's true, she thought to herself. Carl was to be pitied. How very tragic to never see his successful son, his lovely daughter-in-law, his beautiful grandchildren. It was his loss, not hers.

She found herself–also for the first time–actually feeling sorry for her mother-in-law who must surely have passed away by now. What pain, what hurt, what experiences had she had that had formed her into such a fearful, possessive and overbearing woman?

Janet fell asleep that night with a fresh appreciation for the joy her family gave her. She was so proud of Tom. She thought of Julie and of Julie's son. She wondered where he was. What was he doing with his life? Was he married? Did he have children? She fervently hoped he did.

And whatever happened to Brian? Was he, like Carl, forever deprived of experiencing the unique joy that only grandchildren can give?

She thought again of the young man who'd caught her eye on the street, then chided herself for indulging silly imaginations. She rolled over and within minutes was fast asleep.

A few miles away, Carmela lay wide awake, thinking about Janet, thinking about Julie and reviewing in her mind the story Janet had shared with her three days earlier. She hadn't been able to get it off her mind.

Chapter 10
Cecilia's Surprise

"We can't let her cook," Carmela pontificated. "She can set the most beautiful table in Florence, but the food she puts on it–Mama mia, British bland to the max!"

Janet, Paula Jean and Carmela were on their way to lunch at Cecilia's who had informed her friends the day before that she wanted their help in planning a dinner party.

"Who is it again that's coming?" Paula Jean asked.

"The parents of my son and daughter-in-law's new friends. They're from England and his parents are coming to Italy for the first time for a visit," Janet replied. "I haven't met the young couple yet but Tom and Jennifer speak very highly of them. He's in the hotel business and was offered a great job in Florence–one of the fancy hotels but I don't recall which one."

"OK," Paula Jean paused., "but what's the connection with Cecilia?" She looked curiously at Janet.

Chuckling, Janet replied, "Oh, I don't know. Probably because they're from England and she enjoys setting a grand table with all her china and sterling. She does do the 'pomp and circumstance' thing real well, even in a small Italian cottage."

"But it's lovely," Paula Jean retorted a bit defensively.

"I didn't mean that negatively," Janet reacted quickly. "I think it's lovely, too. It's just so different to what I've been used to all my life. You know me–soda fountain glasses and Pfaltzgraff stoneware. Sturdy and durable, that's about as fancy as I get."

"I'm with you," Carmela quipped as she turned the car into Cecilia's driveway. "I like easy and simple."

Cecilia, attired in a tailored navy blue dress, low-heeled Mary Jane's in the same color and her trademark white pearls, looked every bit the British Lady. She welcomed them with a warm smile. First through the door, Paula Jean threw her arms around Cecilia in a typical southern style hug. Janet followed suit and Carmela kissed Cecilia on both cheeks, asking, "Are you used to this yet?" Cecilia reddened slightly. "Slowly, slowly," she answered demurely.

Carmela, Janet and Paula Jean had all come from North America where hugging was quite normal among friends and acquaintances. At first Cecilia had found such demonstrations of affection quite strange and rather uncomfortable, given her more reserved British upbringing. She had warmed up considerably in the past year and was even seen to initiate a hug recently at one of their gatherings.

The table was exquisite as always. The tablecloth of burgundy linen was an exact match to the hue of the roses that adorned the Royal Albert china. The napkins were of the same linen and the Waterford crystal goblets sparkled. In the center of the round table was Cecilia's matching Waterford vase, filled with an elegant arrangement of flowers picked that morning from her garden. The vase was one of her most treasured possessions, a gift she'd received from her late husband on her fortieth birthday. Paula Jean was the first to notice the scrumptious looking cake displayed on Cecilia's sideboard. "Wow," she exclaimed, "did you make that?"

Cecilia nodded shyly. "I did, actually. I made it last night and glazed it this morning."

"Can we skip lunch and go straight to desert?" Carmela proposed. Cecilia responded with a typical British school-marm look, head tilted down, raised eyes peering over the top of her glasses. "No we can't," she said authoritatively but with a smile. "I have a surprise for you—for all of you. Please, go ahead and sit down," she finished smugly.

Cecilia disappeared into the kitchen while the three women settled into their usual places at her table. Moments later, she came back carrying a silver tray on which there were four steaming bowls of soup. She carefully set it down at one end of the sideboard then served each bowl of soup and explained in quite a formal voice, "Our first course this afternoon, ladies, is Tuscany Bean Soup with Basil Pesto. I'll bring the Focaccia in just a moment." Cecilia was obviously enjoying her friends' shocked expressions. Disappearing into the kitchen, she returned with a basket of focaccia and a small bowl with olive oil and spices for dipping.

She took her seat, looked around at her friends, smiled and said, "Bon Appetit!" With that, she dipped her spoon into the soup bowl at her place and brought it to her mouth. The others just stared. This was *not* the norm for lunch at Cecilia's. They had come to expect a limited variety that included offerings like Egg and Cress sandwiches or Fish Fingers with Chips and Mushy Peas.

"Is it your birthday? Did we forget something?" Paula Jean ventured.

Cecilia could contain herself no longer. She burst out laughing as Janet, Carmela and Paula Jean just looked at her.

Still laughing, she wiped her mouth and looked around the table. "If you could just see your faces...." She laughed heartily again before composing herself.

"You can't imagine how long I've been planning this, " she began, as she giggled.

Carmela shook her head with a smile. "What have you been up to, Cecilia?" she asked.

Taking a deep breath, Cecilia replied, "OK, time to 'fess up, as they say. I know you ladies have never been very impressed with my simple English way of eating and cooking." Paula Jean glanced over at Carmela and grinned.

"A few months ago I decided that I was going to learn to cook some different kinds of foods that I've never eaten before, much less cooked. So I bought myself an Italian cookbook, in English of course, at the bookstore in town. Then I went on the internet and ordered a book on French Cooking as well as a Betty Crocker. I even ordered a book on Mexican cooking. How about that, Carmela?" Cecilia winked at her friend. Carmela's eyes opened wide in disbelief.

"So I started with the Italian one and picked out a few recipes that I thought might be—well—edible for a Brit," she chuckled. "I tried them out on a small scale, just for me and to my surprise, I liked them. So I tried a few more. When the books from Amazon came, I started experimenting with some more recipes. I had a few flops along the way and a few that were actually awful, but overall, I discovered that there is life beyond Shepherd's Pie and Yorkshire Pudding. What do you think of that?"

Carmela, Janet and Paula Jean broke into spontaneous applause accompanied by hilarious laughter.

"Incredible!" exclaimed Janet. "I never would have believed it!"

"You are something else," cried Carmela. "You–with a Mexican cookbook? Tell me, did you try to make Tamales?"

Cecilia lowered her head and giggled. "Yes, I did, but they ended up in the rubbish. They were awful. I haven't tried again yet. I decided Tamales would wait until I revealed my secret project to all of you, then you could help me the next time I want to try making Tamales."

Ever the one deeply sensitive to the feelings of others, Paula Jean addressed Cecilia, "This is wonderful, but I hope that we never made you feel bad about your cooking or what you served us. I would feel terrible if we made you uncomfortable."

"Not at all," Cecilia responded. "That's sweet of you to say that, but I was never offended. Look, I'm a realist. I know my cooking was boring. The British have never been known for their cuisine. I just finally decided that I should do something about it and I have you three to thank for it. You are the ones who introduced me to all sorts of foods that I'd never indulged in before moving here. You sparked my interest so my adventure in cooking is my tribute to all of you," she concluded.

"So," she continued, "today's lunch is an international event. And, it's a trial run for the dinner party. Shall I tell you the rest of the menu?"

"By all means," Paula Jean nodded.

"After the soup, there's Greek salad the way the Greeks really make it. In Greece, I learned, Greek salad has no lettuce. It's just cucumbers, tomatoes, red onion, olives and Feta cheese sprinkled lightly with some herbs.

The main course is French–Coq au Vin with fruited rice, steamed broccoli with a lemon sauce and French bread.

Gesturing towards the sideboard, she added, "For dessert we have Grande Marnier Cake with a Chocolate Ganache and, she hesitated dramatically, something you *haven't* seen: Cinnamon Churros."

"You're kidding,' Carmela nearly shrieked. "You made Cinnamon Churros?" At that Carmela got up from her seat, came around the table and pulled Cecilia into a big hug, laughing the whole time. Janet broke out into an exuberant rendition of "For she's a jolly good fellow..." Paula Jean joined right in.

As the shock of Cecilia's surprise dissipated, the women finished off their soup, raving about it. The Greek salad was not only delicious but beautifully presented. Cecilia showed them the photo in the cookbook which she used as her guide. Her salads looked exactly like the picture. The women lingered over the salad, sipping a white Italian wine which Cecilia had purchased for the occasion.

They asked question after question, wanting to hear every detail of Cecilia's private cooking adventure. They laughed til they cried when she described her difficulty in cutting up a mango for the first time. It was a very relaxed lunch. No one was in a hurry.

They ooh-ed and aah-ed over the Coq Au Vin and the fruited rice. Paula Jean, who loved everything lemon, raved about the sauce on the broccoli and refused to leave for home later until she had a copy of the recipe.

After the main course, Janet suggested a break before dessert. They all agreed and helped Cecilia clear the table. With wine glasses replenished, they moved to the living room to discuss the upcoming dinner party.

Cecilia had a notebook handy in which she had already listed a variety of menu options. The Tuscany Bean soup was magnificent, Paula Jean said, but felt that perhaps for the dinner party, a lighter soup would be better. Cecilia quickly suggested Cold Strawberry soup and the others agreed.

They decided to keep the Greek salad on the menu and chose Lasagna for the main course. "Nothing against the Coq au Vin," Janet was quick to remark, " it was fantastic. I just think that Lasagna is such a widely loved dish and goes a long way."

Carmela agreed and Cecilia commented that she had "perfected" a homemade marinara sauce and therefore felt capable of making the Lasagna.

It was one surprise after another. The more they discussed the dinner party, the more they realized how much effort Cecilia had invested during the past few months expanding her cooking knowledge and skills. They were deeply impressed.

When Cecilia suggested making her Focaccia to accompany the Lasagna, Carmela interjected, "Cecilia, I am still in shock at what you've done. I just want to say I'm so proud of you. You're amazing." Paula Jean and Janet echoed, "Me, too."

"Thanks," Cecilia said shyly. "It's been more fun than I ever thought it could be. It's opened up a whole new world for me. I meant what I said before–thank you."

An hour later, Cecilia had the dinner party planned to the minutest detail. They all wanted to contribute in some way so in the end, Carmela was assigned the Strawberry Soup and Cinnamon Churros, Paula Jean agreed to make the Greek salad—"exactly as I made it" Cecilia insisted–and Janet would provide the wine and a fruit and cheese platter to be served between the main course and dessert. The Lasagna and the Grand Marnier cake, as well as arranging and decorating the table, Cecilia took on herself. Cecilia also insisted on making the focaccia.

With enough time having passed since the main course to enable them to enjoy the dessert, the four friends returned to the table where delicate cake plates and sterling silver cake forks were set at each place along with the matching china tea cups and saucers. Cecilia brought out a cut glass platter piled high with Cinnamon Churros and she moved the cake from the sideboard and set it down alongside the platter.

If the main course had garnered accolades, the desserts did so even more. The three women found themselves repeating the same words over and over. "This was amazing..." or "I'm still stunned..." or "I'm so impressed, Cecilia..."

They lingered over tea for another hour or so, savoring the special feeling of this particular lunch experience. Cecilia beamed. She looked around at her friends with nothing but happy thoughts and warm feelings. *I have so much to be thankful for*, she mused.

The ringing of Janet's cell phone broke into their relaxed conversation. It was Jennifer, confirming that Janet would babysit for her and Tom a few days later.

Janet told her about Cecilia's food adventure and assured her that Tom's parents would be treated to an elegant and delicious meal.

The dinner party was set for two weeks later, a few days after Taylor's parents arrived in Italy. Tom and Jennifer were invited as well. Catherine was arranging a baby sitter at the Broderick's home and the Bradshaw children were all invited for

a sleep over the night of the adults' dinner party. The children were elated.

The next morning, Carmela called Janet. "I had a hard time sleeping last night," she began. "I can't get over what Cecilia did. She's amazing."

"Absolutely," Janet agreed. "I woke up during the night thinking about her and couldn't get back to sleep. The work she put in, the time. And she was so happy last night, wasn't she? She's always been so quiet, kind of reserved. I don't think I've ever seen her as vibrant as she was last night. It was so nice to see, wasn't it?"

"Do you remember what I said in the car on the way over?" Carmela continued.

" 'We can't let her cook'. Wow, did I have to eat those words."

"Don't feel too bad," Janet replied. "We've all felt the same way but not anymore."

Carmela hesitated, then said, "Janet, I also keep thinking about your sister and that whole situation."

Janet was quiet for a few moments. "Thanks, Carmela," she said softly. "I think about it a lot, too. Thanks for not thinking I'm crazy."

"Not at all, my friend," Carmela answered. "Life is funny sometimes. Stranger things have happened. I'm a firm believer that if something is meant to be, it will be."

The rest of the morning, Carmela's words ran through Janet's mind, "If something is meant to be, it will be." *She's right*, Janet thought to herself. *I need to stop thinking about it so much. I'm sure it's impossible. It just can't be.*

But somewhere deep inside, she didn't really believe what she was saying to herself.

Chapter 11
A Critical Decision

"Not again," Paula Jean moaned. "When is he going to get it?"

She dropped the notecard onto the hall table, sighing in frustration. She was getting tired of Ferko's stubbornness.

When he first re-entered her life after so many years, they had enjoyed a few dinners out, a movie here and there. It was relaxed, easy, and seemed to be comfortable, a mature friendship. At least that's what it was for Paula Jean, but it didn't take long for Ferko's real intentions to come to the surface. He was still "desperately, insanely in love" with her, he insisted. "After all the years we've lost, why not enjoy the last years of our lives together? Why not reclaim some of our lost youth?"

Paula Jean had pronounced a definitive 'No' the first time he asked her to marry him, but if Ferko was anything, he was persistent. He let a couple of weeks go by and then showed up one evening with a huge bouquet of red roses and a bottle of wine. It so happened that Paula Jean was particularly weary that evening since she'd worked outside in her garden most of the day. About to draw a warm bath preparatory to retiring early, the last thing she wanted when he showed up at her door was to have to entertain Ferko, especially since she already knew he tended to stay as long as possible whenever he visited. Much to his dismay, Paula Jean ushered him out ten minutes after he arrived, telling him truthfully that she was extremely tired.

A few days later he came bearing white roses and tickets to the Opera. He had it all planned. "I've made reservations for dinner at 7 tomorrow night which will give us plenty of time to get to the 9 pm performance at the Opera," he announced.

"But, Ferko," Paula Jean replied, "I already have plans for tomorrow evening."

"So cancel them," he promptly responded.

"Just a minute," Paula Jean bristled. "No, I can't cancel them. I made a commitment that I intend to keep."

"Well, wherever you're going, I'll come with you. I can exchange the Opera tickets..."

"Excuse me, Ferko," Paula Jean was getting heated, "you don't waltz in here and start taking over my life. First of all, you're not invited where I'm going tomorrow evening, and it's incredibly rude to assume..."

Ferko interrupted, "But, darling, I just want to be with you." His voice was cajoling. "I love you so much."

Paula Jean was not moved. She was annoyed.

"Ferko," she tried to speak calmly. "For the umpteenth time, you cannot just sally back into my life after fifty years and expect me to drop everything and everyone and be totally consumed with you. It's not realistic and it's not going to happen."

"But darling," he objected. "Why? Why should we continue our separate lives when destiny has brought us back together after all these years?" He looked at her intently.

"Destiny?" she repeated. "I'm not so sure that it's destiny; maybe it's just an opportunity to bring closure to a fantasy."

Ferko's demeanor changed. "How can you say such a thing?" he demanded rather harshly. "Do you have any idea what it cost me to find you?"

"No, I don't," she admitted, "because you've never told me. When I asked you how you managed to locate me, you evaded the question. So, how *did* you find me?" She crossed her arms and squared her shoulders.

At that moment, Ferko's cell phone rang and he looked at the screen. "Just a minute, darling," he spoke more softly. "I have to take this." He turned and stepped out on her front porch. Paula Jean was grateful for the break in the conversation. She hated confrontations but she wasn't about to put up with his domineering ways.

She also didn't like the fact that whenever his cell phone rang he went into another room to answer it.

She took a deep breath, closed her eyes and waited.

The screen door creaked as he stepped back inside. He came towards her with his arms open. "I have to go, I'm sorry. We'll have to talk some more another time." He drew her to him as he spoke, planted a kiss on each cheek, said a rather quick 'I love you' and turned to leave.

"Just like that," Paula Jean asserted. "In the middle of our conversation, you just pick up and leave because your phone rings. No reason, no explanation, yet you expect me to cancel my life to be at your disposal whenever you want." She was indignant and he knew it.

"I'm sorry," was all he said as he went out the door.

Two weeks had passed with no word from Ferko. Paula Jean made no effort to contact him. She toyed with the idea of talking the situation over with Carmela but hadn't done it yet. Now this...

Paula Jean picked up the note card and read the message again.
My dearest,
You may not be able to understand but I truly am sorry that our last visit ended with such strain. I must return to Budapest for a couple of weeks to take care of some business. Perhaps while I'm gone, you will miss me and have a more favorable disposition towards me on my return.
Ever loving you,
Ferko

Grabbing her jacket and keys, Paula Jean headed out to her car. Suddenly she turned around, ran back in the house and stuffed the notecard into her purse. Pulling her cell phone from her purse, she dialed Carmela, praying her friend was home. Ten minutes later, she pulled up in the driveway behind Carmela's Volvo.

"Coffee or tea?" Carmela asked as she pulled two mugs from the kitchen cabinet.

"I'm so glad you showed up. I was looking for an excuse to take a break from my cleaning," Carmela grinned.

"I've been putting this off for a little while, but I really need to talk to you about Ferko," Paula Jean began. "It's getting messy."

Carmela listened attentively but said nothing as she offered Paula Jean some of her freshly baked banana bread. "Just a small piece," Paula Jean said absent-mindedly.

"Let's go out on the veranda," Carmela suggested. "It's such a beautiful day."

"I feel ridiculously stupid," Paula Jean began when the two women were comfortably seated outdoors.

"Well that's one thing that you are *not!*" Carmela replied firmly. "What's going on?"

Over the next half hour, Paula Jean rehearsed for Carmela the saga of her interactions with Ferko from his first appearance at her door to the present.

"He was completely charming at first, like the Ferko I remembered," she noted at one point. "But the more I'm around him, the less I like him," she concluded. "He's getting more and more possessive and demanding. I don't like it, Carmela." She took a bite of the banana bread. "Yum," she purred, "delicious as always."

"He's asked me three times now to marry him," she pressed on, "and each time I've said 'No' as firmly as I know how and he just won't give up. It's getting frustrating. I thought we could just be friends for awhile; you know, get to know each other for who we are now, and not have an agenda. I certainly had no intentions of every marrying again anyway but truthfully, the thought did cross my mind early on that maybe–just maybe–it might happen." She shook her head, "The thought of it now makes me shudder!"

She reached for her purse, pulled out the card and handed it to Carmela. "Today I got this in the mail," she continued. "Not a word for two weeks and then this. I can't shake the feeling that he's very secretive about his life and his dealings but he wants to know everything about me. It's really making me uncomfortable."

Carmela read the note then handed it back to Paula Jean with no comment. She looked into the distance for a few moments as the two women sat, breathing in the quiet of the countryside.

Finally, Carmela turned towards Paula Jean and spoke. "First of all, I'm really glad you came over. I've been troubled for a little while about you and Ferko. Felt like I was seeing some indications I didn't like but I didn't want to butt into your business, you know." She paused. "But I could tell you weren't happy. I noticed the other day at Cecilia's that in the middle of all our hilarity over her cooking, there was a time or two that you looked like you were far away. You weren't *there*, if you know what I mean. I caught it. I knew something was bothering you and I thought it was probably about Ferko."

Another pause, punctuated only by the hum of the bumblebees in Carmela's garden.

"What do you think you should do?" Carmela asked softly, looking intently at Paula Jean.

"I need to be true to myself," Paula Jean answered thoughtfully. "This relationship is going nowhere and I don't need this in my life."

She stretched her legs out in front of her and slid down a bit in the padded chair. "You know, Carmela," she pressed on, "I've always believed that everything happens for a reason. There has to have been a reason for Ferko to show up after all this time. I don't know what the reason is, and right now that may not even be important."

She looked off into the distance.

"What I do know," she said after a brief silence, "is that my life still has purpose but that purpose doesn't include Ferko." She gave a little laugh. "There, I said it. I've known it for a little while but I hadn't quite acknowledged it out loud."

Carmela smiled warmly at her friend. "Maybe the reason isn't as much about you as it is about Ferko. That's possible," Carmela offered. "I think sometimes things happen in our life for the sake of other people. It's not always about us. We're just the agents, if you will."

"Hmm," Paula Jean murmured. "Hadn't thought of it that way. You could be right."

They sat in silence a bit longer, breathing in the serenity of their surroundings.

Paula Jean turned to Carmela, "What did you mean by 'indications'? What were you sensing? Do you want to tell me?"

"It probably doesn't matter anymore. You've made your decision, haven't you?"

"I have, but I have a lot of respect for you, Carmela. I value your insight. I trust you, " Paula Jean said seriously. "I'd like to know what you thought."

"It's not so much what I thought, as a gut feeling. Call it intuition, maybe. From the first time I met Ferko, there was just something I couldn't quite put my finger on. I still don't know what it is exactly, but there's something that makes me uncomfortable. I don't feel that I can trust him. It's the kind of feeling that when I was younger I'd think maybe there was something wrong with me. But as I've gotten older, I've learned to trust those instincts. Something just isn't quite right. That probably doesn't help much, but I don't know how else to say it," Carmela concluded.

"Thank you," Paula Jean whispered. "I know you're right."

Brightening up, Carmela changed the subject. "What are you going to wear to the dinner party at Cecilia's?"

"I don't know. What are you going to wear?" Paula Jean retorted.

"Listen to us," Carmela laughed a hearty laugh. "We sound like teenagers for heaven's sake!" She stood up and in a sing-song voice, chanted, "What are you going to wear to the party tomorrow?"

Paula Jean left for home a short time later. She caught herself humming a happy tune while she drove the short distance and realized she hadn't done that in quite some time. There was a fresh lightness in her soul and a new spring in her step.

She knew what she was going to do when Ferko returned from Budapest. She slept more peacefully that night than she had in several weeks, totally unaware that some five hundred and fifty miles away, events were unfolding that rendered her decision far more critical than she could have possibly imagined.

Chapter 12
The Other Face of Ferko

Ferko was pleased to see that the flight to Paris was half empty. His aisle seat in a center section of three seats was close to the front of the economy cabin. He noted with pleasure the distance between himself and the rear of the cabin where four families with children were trying unsuccessfully to quiet their clamoring offspring. He detested rambunctious children and subscribed to the old adage that 'children were to be seen not heard.'

Once airborne, Ferko stretched his stocky frame across the additional two seats, fussed with the standard issue airline pillow and pulled the thin blanket up to his chin. He preferred these night flights when he could sleep. In his opinion, they were far better than wasting perfectly good daylight strapped into an uncomfortable seat for three or four hours and sometimes longer. Tonight's flight was just under two hours, barely long enough for a reasonable nap but Ferko wanted to sleep. He needed to be alert and sharp on arrival at Charles de Gaulle International Airport.

The cloud cover was thick and landings at De Gaulle Airport were delayed. Ferko's plane circled for nearly an hour before the pilot's voice over the loudspeaker alerted the passengers that they were finally cleared to land. Five minutes later, the plane barely jolted as they touched down. With no checked baggage to claim, Ferko made it through passport control and out of the terminal within thirty minutes. His usual driver was waiting for him. *"Bon soir, Monsieur. Bienvenue a Paris."* It was just past midnight.

Paris, beautiful Paris, Ferko mused to himself as the taxi wove through the familiar streets of the magical city. The drive from the airport to his destination normally took about an hour, even longer in heavy traffic. At this hour traffic was light by Paris standards. Pierre, his driver, pulled up in front of the nondescript house in the

19th *arondissement* in less than 50 minutes and smiled broadly as Ferko paid the fare and added a generous tip. *"Merci beaucoup, Monsieur, Merci,"* Pierre acknowledged. Ferko tipped his hat and disappeared into the building.

He turned the key quietly and closed the door silently, hoping not to wake her but he should have known better. She was waiting for him, as she always did. Her ears were tuned to his arrival. She was never sure exactly when he would return home, so she waited, night after night, for the nearly imperceptible sound of his key in the latch.

Her smile was genuine, her loyalty unswerving. He was her hero, her first and only love, her husband of thirty-eight years, the father of her two fine sons. *France had its great king, Francois I,* she liked to say to her few friends, *but my Francois is better than ten kings.* She adored him. He could do no wrong in her eyes.

The aroma of freshly baked bread lingered in the small apartment, illuminated by a single antique lamp in the corner of the dusty living room. Ferko kissed his wife gently. She told him the soup was hot and the table was prepared. "I'll be there in a moment," he called back as he took his satchel into the bedroom.

"How was Milan?" she asked, after they were seated. "Did your dealings go well?"

"Oh, very well indeed," Ferko replied with a beguiling smile. It had long since ceased bothering him that he lived a continual lie. "Soon we'll be able to pay off all our debts and then, what shall we do? A new apartment? Perhaps in the south of France where it's warmer? Would that make you happy, *ma Cherie?*" She clapped her hands like a little girl and giggled like a teenager.

Though she was only sixty-two, she appeared much older. The unrelenting stress of poor health, financial worries and Ferko's frequent long absences for "business trips" during all the years of their marriage had taken its toll on Marquerite. Her auburn curls, so attractive to Ferko when she was young, were now grey and dull. Her skin was yellowed and wrinkled from years of smoking too many cigarettes and drinking far too much French wine, usually at home by herself night after night. She had a chronic cough that no medication alleviated and she was hopelessly thin.

Hers had been a lonely life. Her boys had filled her days with work and pleasure when they were young, but she barely saw them now. Francois Michel, the eldest, lived and worked in London. He rarely came back to visit though London was just a two hour train ride away. Like his father before him, he was always "away on business."

Philippe, the younger son, was an artist, living in New York. Marguerite hadn't seen him in four years.

And Ferko? *Well,* she told herself, *he works so hard to make a living. I mustn't complain.* She loved him blindly, naively, irrevocably. A few years earlier when a friend of hers raised certain doubts about Ferko's constant travelling, Marguerite was incensed. How dare Liliana suggest that there was anything untoward about Ferko's hard work? She never spoke to Liliana again.

"The soup is delicious, *ma Cherie.* Is there more?" Ferko asked, handing her his bowl. She shuffled to the stove and ladled out another serving. Ferko tore off another hunk of bread and dipped it in olive oil.

"How long will you be home this time?" she asked hesitantly. "I would love for you to take me to the *Jardin des Plantes* if you have time." The Royal Botanical Garden was her favorite site in all of Paris. She'd had a passionate love of flowers and plants since she was a child.

"Mmm," Ferko grunted. Wiping his mouth with a napkin, he added, "I'm sure we can do that. Maybe tomorrow?"

"If the weather's good," she replied. Marguerite's fragile health was very sensitive to extremes in temperature and she never went out in the rain for fear of catching cold. Her *docteur pneumologue* had warned her against it.

The following morning dawned grey and cold. Dark clouds promised rain and windy gusts rattled the brittle window frames of the old apartment. Ferko was up early, showered in tepid water, cursing the ancient plumbing of the miserable building. After breakfast he told Marguerite he needed to check in at his office and would be back about lunch time. He left her curled up under a heavy woolen blanket on the faded sofa. He had turned on the television for her, a thirty year old nineteen inch model whose picture faded in and out at will and whose sound was scratchy at best. All it really provided was noise to distract her from the lonely silence in the house. It certainly was not a source of entertainment.

Ferko walked quickly, always vigilant of his surroundings. In minutes he reached his first destination, a small framing shop tucked in a narrow alley between apartment houses. A harsh bell sounded when he opened the door and stepped inside. From behind a heavy curtain, a small man with stooped shoulders poked his head out and seeing Ferko, scowled and said, "You're too early. Come back later." He disappeared behind the curtain as Ferko protested.

"Jacques, it was supposed to be ready last night. I want it now."

"Go away," came the muffled words. Ferko darted behind the counter, thrust his hand into the opening in the curtain and pulled it roughly back. The small man was standing next to an old metal file cabinet, peering at Ferko over the rim of his spectacles that hung precariously close to the end of his nose.

"These things take time, Francois," the man named Jacques barked. "You want it done right, don't you?"

Ferko swore under his breath. "When?" he demanded.

"Come back this afternoon. Now go!" Jacques said with an icy stare.

Ferko's next stop was two blocks further down, another hole-in-the-wall type place. This one sported a square weathered sign, *Magasin de Bagage*. The luggage on display looked early vintage and the overall appearance of the shop was 1950-ish. Years of accumulated street dust gave the front window a smoky look. The shop was dark.

Ferko tried the door but it was locked. Looking up and down the street, he took one step closer and jiggled the doorknob violently, once, twice, three times. Moments later, a stringy haired young man peered out through the peephole of the shop's door, recognized Ferko and demanded, but not too loudly, *Mot de passe?* [password]

Ferko promptly answered, *"Marie Antoinette"*.

The door opened and Ferko swept by the young man with not so much as a *"Bonjour."* He continued straight ahead, past the service counter and through a narrow door which opened up on a large room behind the partition. Four scratched and battered wooden desks were positioned in a cluster at the center of the room. Each one had a state of the art laptop chained to a beam that ran the length of the low ceiling. At three of the desks, sloppily dressed, middle-aged men with headphones were clicking away on computer keys, oblivious of each other or anyone else in the room. Not even one looked up to acknowledge Ferko's arrival.

In front of the far wall was a long wooden table on which was a bank of the most up to date computers and laser printers, whirring away and rapidly spitting out printed pages.

Along the adjoining wall was a large table with a coffee urn, assorted cracked and stained porcelain mugs, an open bag of sugar and a jug, presumably of milk. This was *le bureau*, "the office."

Ferko went straight to the coffee urn, poured himself a cup and laced it with 2 heaping spoons of sugar. Carrying it to the single unoccupied desk in the center of the room, he sat down, took a sip of his coffee, then fired up the laptop in front of him. Moments later, he was scrolling through long lists of names. Occasionally he stopped on a particular name, made an illegible note on a yellow pad and resumed scrolling.

An hour later, he exited the screen he'd been working on, rebooted the laptop and entered 'Paula Jean Jackson' into an unusual search tab. Working quickly through a network of proxy servers, he hacked into Paula Jean's bank account in Alabama as well as her account in Florence. He smiled a knowing smile.

At precisely 11:30 am, everyone in the room stopped working. Headphones were removed, printers were silenced, and Ferko greeted his co-workers.

"Good work," he began. "We're in good shape," he said in flawless French. "By this time next month, we should be able to close up shop and go enjoy our acquired wealth."

The others grinned confidently. They had been running this scam for nearly three years and had successfully swindled many a healthy widow in more than 7 European countries. The innocent victims slept better at night, believing they had elite insurance coverage, with no deductible, against any future need for nursing home care. And more importantly in their eyes, their children's inheritance was protected for this 'new' policy stipulated that the insured's personal financial assets could not be tapped for nursing home or medical care. It was all written clearly in the policy. What could be better?

The other three men, like Ferko, lived in very modest apartments. None of the four had yet personally tasted the better life. All their ill-gotten profits were hidden away in four different offshore accounts under false names taken from false passports which all of them possessed. They had agreed from the beginning to control their greed, to exercise disciplined patience as they waited for the pre-determined end date for their 'project', as they called it. Then each of them would disappear and with yet another identity, start a new life in some exotic destination. It was foolproof. Even their wives–no, especially their wives–had no idea what they were doing and the four of them had collaborated to create intricate cover stories to explain each of their projected international moves when the time came.

But Ferko had a problem that the others didn't. His was not simply a double life. Besides Marguerite and his sons, there was also Regina in the south of France, Tatiana in Prague, Maria in Barcelona. And presently he had added into the mix the love of his youth, Paula Jean, the only one of his entourage of women that had actually maintained a lasting presence in his mind for all fifty odd years.

Yet he was prepared to make her a victim as well, though not with the insurance scam. He had realized weeks ago that she was far too sharp to be fooled as others had been by his elaborate scheme. He had to tread carefully with Paula Jean. She was American and he knew that American women tended to be far more educated in such matters, unlike the more naïve European women he had defrauded. The European female seniors he targeted were widows of husbands who'd handled all their affairs and left their wives to tend to womanly things. When their husbands died, most of them hardly knew how to read a bank statement. None of them had worked outside the home. Those were the women he liked. To be sure, times were changing in Europe but when he conceived his plan, it had not been difficult to find enough women of the old school mentality to provide him with the amount of money he had projected would give him a more than comfortable retirement, complete with the funds to 'keep' as many women as he fancied. This was his final stab at real wealth after being a colossal failure in business over the previous decades. He'd spent months devising his plan and chose his "co-workers" with extreme shrewdness.

Their 'work' for the day completed, each of the men left separately. Ferko was last. He double-checked the rear door's triple lock, made sure the dark curtain on the single small window of their 'office' completely covered the window, triple locked the front door, and after checking that the immediate area was clear, walked quickly towards home.

He'd promised Marguerite he'd stay in Paris for two weeks and he kept his word. He feigned vacation time and took Marguerite to her favorite cafes, wined and dined her in her favorite restaurants and accompanied her not once, but twice, to the Jardin des Plantes. More than once, she asked him if they could afford all these outings and he smiled, patted her hand and assured her he had saved for over a year to be able to treat her to these pleasures. Marguerite beamed with pleasure. *He really loves me,* she prattled to herself. She never would have believed that behind his loving smile, he thought her a bore and a stupid old woman. She would never know the truth about Ferko. He would make sure of that.

While she reveled in the beauty of the gardens, his thoughts turned to Paula Jean. Her bank balances were *magnifique,* better than anything he could have hoped for. Jack had provided superbly for her. Marriage to Paula Jean was the only way he could see to achieve his ends. He would dip into his secret account, buy her a diamond ring no woman could refuse and marry her quickly. He made a mental note to slip out to the frame shop after taking Marguerite home. The new set of false documents were ready and waiting.

Mmm, he mused to himself. *Paula Jean–all that money.* He could hardly wait to get his hands on it.

Chapter 13
The Dinner Party

Cecilia's home was a beehive of activity. It had started at 8 am when Janet swept through the front door, finding Cecilia still in her pajamas, her oversized coffee mug in her right hand and a mop in her left.

"Put me to work," Janet declared. "What do you need done?" Cecilia pointed to a soft rag and a bottle of silver polish on the dining room sideboard. "The candlesticks need a touch up and please check the flatware. Some of the pieces may need a bit of polish as well."

"How many are we in the end?" Janet inquired.

"Ten. I need to get two extra chairs from the guest room and we'll need to insert all the leaves to my table. But let's get the cleaning finished first."

Cecilia had actually been cleaning for several days. When she tired of the physical exertion, she'd retreat to the kitchen for a break. The rear wall of Cecilia's kitchen was curved as there was a floor to ceiling bay window that overlooked the back garden. Into the nook formed by the bay, she'd placed her antique rocking chair, a small bookcase, the top shelf of which now held her newly acquired cookbook collection, and a floor lamp with a curved upper arm to facilitate reading. There was also a small side table, permanently equipped with a coaster to hold her tea cup and whatever book she was reading at the moment. It was her relaxation corner, but not today.

She'd baked the lasagna the night before, explaining to Janet that according to her cookbook, lasagna was much better the second day after time enhanced the flavors. Janet smiled dutifully. The dough for the focaccia was rising in a warm spot and as soon as the tile floors in the front hall, living room and dining room were mopped, she was going to get dressed in her *sloppies,* as she called her work clothes, and begin preparing the dining room table.

"What about the cake?" Janet looked over at Cecilia.

"Once the focaccia is in the oven, I'll start on it. I want to get the table ready so that while I'm mixing the cake, you can start setting out the china."

"Are you sure you don't want Paula Jean to do that?" Janet teased. "She's the only other one of us that even has china."

"I heard that," chimed Paula Jean, walking into the room, followed by Carmela who was carrying a large pot. Paula Jean dropped her purse on the floor by the corner of the sideboard as Carmela walked on into the kitchen saying, "Where do you want the strawberry soup? Is there room in your fridge?"

Paula Jean went back out to the car to get the Greek salad she had prepared and the large Tupperware container with Carmela's Cinnamon Churros. Cecilia pronounced the salad "absolutely perfect" and snagged a less than perfectly formed churro to sample. "Um, heavenly."

"But, of course," Carmela feigned surprise. "What did you expect?"

"Where's my sample?" Janet jumped in. "Split one with you," Paula Jean offered.

"Who says I want to split one? Have your own!" Janet laughed. "There's enough for an army here."

"OK, OK," Cecilia chimed in. "Time to get to work. There's coffee made, you know where it is. I've got a list here of what needs to be done. As each of you finish your job, if you'll cross it off the list then we'll be sure not to forget anything. OK with you?" Cecilia looked around.

"Sure thing, Capitano," Carmela saluted.

Like four busy bees, each of the women fell to their tasks. Janet polished the silver to an eye-catching brilliance, then dusted the entire dining room even though it didn't really need it.

Carmela and Paula Jean set the table. Cecilia had brought out her best linen tablecloth and its matching napkins. It was pure white and crisp with the simplest of delicate embroidery down its center. Cecilia was about to give instructions on how she wanted the table set but Carmela interrupted. "I worked at the Savoy in London, remember? Don't worry. I got it covered." Cecilia grinned, "A Mexican with British finesse! Ah! Shakespeare would be proud!" They all laughed as she added, "It's all yours–I'll be in the kitchen if you need me."

By noon, the Grand Marnier cake was cooling on the rack, the dining room looked like a cover photo from Woman & Home magazine and the four women were tired but pleased with the results of their work.

When Cecilia stepped into the dining room to survey Carmela and Paula Jean's efforts, she was in awed at the sight. The Royal Albert China was meticulously arranged, the Waterford crystal goblets and wine glasses gleamed in the sunlight, and the napkins were folded to resemble swans and looked as though they were floating on the salad plates, positioned on top of the dinner plates. Down the center of the table was an exquisite arrangement of candles of various heights in colors that matched the china (of course!). In and out among the candles Paula Jean had woven ribbons of complementary colors which every so often were coaxed into an abstract shape. It was stunning.

Their preparations completed, the four women congregated around Cecilia's kitchen island for lunch. She brought out egg and cress sandwiches and potato chips, "for old times sake", she quipped. A large bowl of fresh fruit and some left over pound cake that Janet had brought along completed the meal.

By two p.m., Janet, Paula Jean and Carmela were on their way to their own homes to have a bit of a rest, shower and dress for the evening. Tom and Jennifer were bringing Taylor and Catherine and Taylor's parents at seven but the women had agreed to be back at Cecilia's by six in case she needed help with anything at the last minute.

Carmela stretched out on her sofa and punched the remote for the television. She knew she wouldn't sleep if she lay on the bed but sometimes the drone of the television did the trick. The news was on which Carmela found boring so she reached for the remote to channel surf for something more appealing. Just as she hit the button to change the channel, something caught her eye. She quickly clicked again to go back to the previous screen. She looked carefully but didn't see anything. She waited for just a minute and was about to dismiss the thought and suddenly, she saw it again.

A reporter was talking into the camera but Carmela paid no attention to him. She was looking behind him into the small crowd to his right. She cocked her head to one side, staring. The camera panned and she noticed the Eiffel Tower in the background.

There he was again—a familiar profile, a familiar walk, an older woman on his arm. She squinted to see more clearly. Suddenly he turned, full face to the camera. She gasped out loud, swung her legs off the couch and leaned forward.

What is he doing in Paris? She said aloud to herself. *He's supposed to be in Budapest.*

Her eyes were glued to the screen. People were walking by, the reporter was still reporting. The man and the old woman disappeared. Carmela continued staring.

Ten seconds or so later, the camera panned again, this time in the opposite direction. There he was, walking away, his back to the camera, the old woman leaning on him.

"It's him, that's him!" she said out loud again. *"What the...? Who the heck is that old woman?"*

The scene disappeared and the news program moved on to another story. Carmela fell back on the sofa cushions and just stared at the ceiling for a long time. Questions raced through her mind, suspicions multiplied, scenarios burst out of her imagination.

Stop it, stop it—right now! She finally ordered herself out loud. *This is ridiculous.*

The possibility of a short nap now completely ruined, Carmela made a cup of tea and settled into her recliner. She picked up a copy of *Endless Summer* which she had borrowed from Janet and tried to read. It was useless. She closed the book, leaned back and allowed her mind to wander wherever it chose. She'd discovered years ago that when she was faced with a problem or a crisis, this approach for some reason worked for her quite often. "God," she murmured, "if that's really Ferko, something's very weird. I just want to ask you to protect Paula Jean. Keep her safe, God. Amen."

An hour later, the ringing of her cell phone woke her up. Janet had taken it upon herself to make sure that Carmela and Paula Jean wouldn't oversleep. While she was a light sleeper who rarely took naps during the day, she knew the other two were not and had been known to dream their way undisturbed through a raging thunderstorm or two.

"Shall I pick you up? No point taking three cars," Janet suggested.

"Thanks," Carmela accepted. "What time?"

"I'll be at Paula Jean's at 5:30 so we'll get to your place shortly afterwards. That good with you?"

"Fine, thanks. See you then." Carmela clicked off. She rubbed her eyes awake, sat up straight. The television was still on so she watched for a few minutes, then clicked it off and made her way to the bathroom.

Royal blue was a great color on Carmela and the three strand pearl necklace set against the deep hue of the two piece dress was an elegant touch. She fluffed up her curly hair and secured her earrings. Looking at herself in the mirror, Carmela mused, *Not so bad for almost 63*. She heard the honk of Janet's car and picking up her purse and wrap, she flipped on a night light in the front hall, set the alarm and went out the front door.

Janet had opted for a fuschia and navy colorblock dress that complimented her trim figure and Paula Jean wore her favorite dove grey pleated skirt with a ruffled petal pink silk blouse. Without planning it ahead of time, they had all chosen to accessorize their outfits with pearls.

"Looks like it's another pearl night," Janet remarked as Carmela slid into the back seat. "It'll be pretty funny if Cecilia is also wearing her pearls. Taylor's parents may think we're the pearl quartet or something."

It was a short ride to Cecilia's who greeted them enthusiastically. "Good choice," Paula Jean exclaimed when Cecilia opened the door. "You look gorgeous."

Cecilia was wearing her favorite dress, a sheath in a rich emerald green that enhanced the color of her hazel eyes. Her white hair was pulled back in a French twist to reveal pearl and diamond earrings. A matching pearl and diamond brooch was fastened to her dress in just the right spot below her left shoulder.

"Look at us," Carmela spoke up. "We're not the "Golden Girls". We're the "Pearl Girls". And don't we all look just soooo elegant!" They all laughed as Cecilia led them into the living room. "Anyone for a pre-dinner glass of wine?"

At 6:45 Carmela ladled the Strawberry Soup into bowls and set them on two trays, ready to serve. Cecilia made a last minute check of everything and ten minutes later, the doorbell rang.

Janet jumped up to open the door then held back to defer to Cecilia. Tom and Jennifer came in first, smiling and hugging each of the women. Catherine was next, followed by an elderly couple, obviously Taylor's parents. "Taylor will be right in. He just had a call from the hotel. The joys of being a hotel manager," Catherine apologized.

Introductions were completed all around just as the door opened to admit Taylor. Tom pulled his friend forward to introduce him. Taylor greeted Cecilia warmly, thanking her for hosting all of them, then turned to Paula Jean. As Taylor lingered briefly talking to Paula Jean, Carmela felt Janet suddenly grab her hand. She squeezed it tightly, very tightly. Carmela turned to look and Janet was white as a sheet. In a flash, she realized what was happening as Janet stared at Taylor.

"This is Carmela," Tom was saying. "If you like spicy food, you really want to get to know this lady. Better than any Mexican restaurant anywhere in Italy," he smiled broadly, bowing towards Carmela. Taylor took both of Carmela's hands in his and said, "We *love* Mexican food, even if we are British!" With that, he laughed heartily and Tom edged him forward towards Janet.

"And this is my Mom, Janet," Taylor embraced Janet warmly and said, "I've heard so many great things about you. It's wonderful to meet you. Did you meet my wife?"

"Yes, she's so lovely," Janet replied. "It's so nice to meet you, too. Tom and Jennifer think the world of you both."

Somehow Janet had managed to pull herself together. Carmela was impressed as she watched her. No one else had any idea what was going on inside Janet's mind and emotions.

The senior Brodericks were shy at first but as the evening wore on, Mrs. Broderick seemed to relax and began to engage more easily in conversation. Mr. Broderick managed rather well considering the Parkinsons. He smiled almost continually though he said little. Taylor and Catherine were effusive in their praise of the food, the décor and the warm environment of the evening. During dessert, Catherine remarked to Janet, "I can see why Jennifer is so happy that you live nearby and that you have these amazing friends. What a warm and wonderful group. I think it's splendid, absolutely splendid."

"So how are you adjusting to Florence," Paula Jean asked, as Cecilia poured the tea. "Are the children doing well?"

"We love it here," Taylor replied immediately. "The kids adjusted very quickly to the new school and they're actually quite excited to be with children from several different countries. They're always coming home with a story about some new custom or tradition they heard about from another child. I think it's a great educational experience for them. Great way to broaden their horizons."

"And I do have to say the weather is a whole lot more pleasant than dreary old England." Catherine winked at her mother-in-law as she said it. The elder Mrs. Broderick smiled in return and nodded her head.

Janet watched the interplay of conversations with keen interest and several times during dinner had to force herself to avert her eyes from staring at Taylor. Once he caught her looking intently at him and she blushed and fiddled with her napkin. It was awkward for a moment but when she looked up, he was asking Cecilia how a born-and-bred British woman was able to concoct such a delectable lasagna.

Janet studied the senior Brodericks and could find no resemblance between Taylor and either of his parents. Before the meal was over, she had concluded that he must have been adopted but she couldn't work out how it could be when the Brodericks had never lived anywhere but on the British Isles. She'd actually asked surreptitiously during the course of the dinner conversation. Mrs. Broderick was proud to tell Janet of her Welsh ancestors and how it came to be that the Broderick clan had settled in Essex.

But he even talks like Brian did, she was thinking. *Could it possibly be?*

She could also see that the Brodericks were intensely proud of their only son and greatly admired their daughter-in-law. They deeply missed the children, Mrs. Broderick confided to Janet, but they don't complain, she said. They don't want Taylor to worry about them.

By 9:30 pm the elder Broderick was getting visibly weary. Taylor glanced at Tom who responded immediately and graciously. Taylor helped his father out of the chair and Catherine slipped her arm through her mother-in-law's. There were hugs and repeated expressions of gratitude all around, more compliments on the meal and five minutes later the much anticipated dinner party was winding down.

Once the guests had left, Janet disappeared into the bathroom. By the time she returned, the table was cleared, Cecilia was putting away the food, and Carmela was loading the dishwasher. Paula Jean was hand washing the goblets and wine glasses as well as the sterling flatware. Janet picked up a dish towel and began to dry the knives and forks. She was very quiet but no one seemed to notice. No one, except Carmela.

Another pot of tea later, Cecilia looked at her friends and said, "I don't know how to thank you. I had such a good time doing this tonight and if it wasn't for you, I never would have attempted it. Thank you so much. I don't think you realize what a big deal it is to me. Not just the dinner party–the whole cooking thing, too." Her eyes were damp.

"It was awesome," Paula Jean asserted. "It really was. We all had a great time."

After dropping Taylor and Catherine and Taylor's parents at the Broderick's home, Tom and Jennifer were driving back to their own place when Jennifer looked over at Tom, then turned her head away. He caught it in his peripheral vision.

"You OK?" he looked over.

"Yeah, sure. It was great tonight."

"Hey, this is me. What's on your mind? Spit it out," he smiled at his wife.

"It was your Mom. Did you notice anything different?"

"Uh, don't think so. Why? Did you?"

Jennifer nodded slowly. "You couldn't see it where you were standing but when Taylor came in and you were introducing him to Cecilia and Paula Jean, I happened to look over at your Mom. Tom, she was white as a sheet–like she'd seen a ghost or something. And I noticed she grabbed Carmela's hand like she was terrified or...I don't know. It was strange."

Tom drove on in silence for a couple of minutes.

"You think she's sick or something?" Tom asked.

"No, I don't think so. She was fine until Taylor came in. Almost like he reminded her of somebody...like a bad memory....something... .I don't know....it was just strange," she repeated.

"So maybe you should just ask her?" Tom suggested.

"Maybe..." Jennifer frowned.

Chapter 14
Cousins

Before dawn the next morning, Janet was sprawled on her living room floor, open cartons on either side of her and another between her legs. She was rifling through file folders and pulling photos out of manila envelopes. Occasionally she lingered with this or that photo, re-living a memory, then pressed on.

Yanking a large photo album out from under a stack of files, she opened it on her lap. Brian and Julie's wedding portrait filled the first page. Her left hand flew to her mouth as she gasped. The deep brown eyes staring at her from the photograph, the wavy hair, the broad smile, even the way he tilted his head... she began to tremble.

It has to be...but how? she whispered to herself, tears welling up. She choked them back and turned page after page, twenty pages in all. She hardly focused on her sister. She was mesmerized by the pictures of Brian. It was Taylor on every page.

She had a sudden thought. *Oh my God*, she breathed aloud. *If Taylor is actually Julie's son, he's Tom's cousin.* A cold chill swept through her body. *Oh, my God, oh my God,* she kept saying to herself.

She spent the morning in a daze. The postman delivered a package she'd been waiting for and she dropped it on the bench near the front door and never opened it. She made herself a second cup of coffee then walked out of the kitchen and forgot to drink it. Her phone rang twice and the sound didn't register. She was in a fog, there but not there.

About one in the afternoon, the phone rang again. It was Jennifer. "Are you on your way?" she asked.

"Uh, on my way?" The tone of Janet's voice alarmed her daughter-in-law.

"Mom, are you OK? You were going to come for lunch today. The children don't have school, remember?"

"Oh, I'm so sorry. I...I got all caught up this morning...um... cleaning out some things. I'll...I'll be there shortly."

Hanging up the phone before Jennifer could say anything else, Janet raced into her bedroom, changed quickly, and brushed her hair. She skipped the makeup routine and applied only a light dab of lipstick. Grabbing her keys and her purse, she headed for the door, pulling her jacket on as she did.

Throughout the twenty minute drive to her children's home, her mind ran on overload. Jennifer was sharp, she was observant and keenly aware of other people's feelings. Janet knew it would be exceedingly difficult to hide her emotions from her daughter-in-law and pretend as if nothing was on her mind. She was two blocks from the house when she made a quick decision. Pulling over to the side of the road, she dialed Carmela. She was about to give up discouraged when Carmela finally answered on the seventh ring.

"I'm on my way to Jennifer's and I don't know what to do," she began.

"Where were you? I've been calling you," Carmela replied.

"You have?" Janet paused. "I was home. I...I found the album... I don't know what to do...if he's my nephew I want him to know... but maybe he won't want to know...do you realize if he is, he's Tom's cousin?"

"Whoa, slow down," Carmela urged. "Why don't you come over?"

"I can't. Jennifer's waiting lunch for me. I forgot...she called.... the kids don't have school. You know how Jennifer is. She'll know I'm upset."

"Janet," Carmela said quietly, "you really need to calm down. This could be a really big deal or it could end up being nothing."

Janet interrupted. "You need to see the pictures. It's him, Carmela. I'm sure of it."

"Ok, look. Try to get through lunch with the grandchildren. Can you talk to Jennifer about it?"

"I don't want to...not yet. Can I bring the photo album over later? I want you to see it."

"I'll be here. Come on over whenever you want to," Carmela assured her.

"Thanks." Janet pushed the button to end the call and sat there for another five minutes, willing herself to relax. By the time she walked into Jennifer's kitchen, she felt somewhat in control. She hugged the children, listened to their latest tidbits of school news, and relished the delicious casserole Jennifer served, realizing she hadn't eaten since the night before and was actually quite hungry.

After the children left the table to go play, Jennifer put on the kettle for tea while Janet cleared the table. Arranging chocolate chip cookies on a glass plate, Jennifer remarked, "Heidi and I made these this morning. I hope they're good. She put twice as many nuts in the batter as it called for."

Janet smiled. "You know how I love chocolate chip cookies."

"Mom," Jennifer looked over at Janet after they'd returned to the table. "Can I ask you something?"

Janet tensed but tried not to show it. "Of course," she replied, looking up.

"Last night...by the way, it was just great. We had the best time and so did our friends. The food was out of this world and Cecilia does such an awesome job at decorating. The table looked amazing, like a upscale London restaurant."

She paused and took a deep breath. "Last night, I noticed something and it's been worrying me every since."

"What's that?" Janet looked curiously at her daughter-in-law.

"I'm worried about you."

Janet conveyed a shocked expression. "Why, darling?"

"I happened to look over at you when Taylor was being introduced. You were white as a sheet. You looked like...I don't know, Mom...like you saw a ghost or something?" She left the question hanging in mid-air. Jennifer's demeanor was intense as her eyes bored into Janet's.

The silence was deafening.

Janet covered her face with her hands. A slow trickle of tears leaked out between her fingers. Jennifer leaned forward and in a hoarse tone, whispered, "Mom, what's wrong?"

No response. Several minutes went by. The ticking of the grandfather clock in the living room was obnoxiously loud all of a sudden.

Janet extended her left hand and gently squeezed Jennifer's arm. "Do you have a tissue?" she asked. Without a word, Jennifer slipped over to the counter, retrieved an open Kleenex box and set it down in front of her mother-in-law.

"I don't know quite how to begin," Janet said finally, blowing her nose for the third time. "It's a really long story."

"Let's go in the living room, Mom," Jennifer urged, taking Janet's arm.

"I don't want to upset the children. Where are they?" Janet questioned.

"Here," Jennifer gestured toward the easy chair. "Why don't you sit here while I go put on a DVD for the children." When she returned, Janet was composed and smiled sadly.

"Sorry," she mumbled. Jennifer shook her head, "It's OK, Mom."

"Do you remember my sister, Julie? I mean, do you remember hearing about her?" Janet began. Jennifer nodded. "She died very young, right?"

"Yes, she did. Do you remember how she died?"

Jennifer wrinkled her forehead and thought for a minute. "No, I'm sorry, I don't."

For the next ten minutes, Janet rehearsed the story, detail by detail, just as she had with Carmela. Jennifer's eyes were glued to her mother-in-law's face and she listened in rapt attention. She didn't move. It seemed at times that she wasn't even breathing, she was so still.

When Janet related how Brian had given away his newborn son, Jennifer gasped out loud and her hands flew to her face. Her eyes were big as saucers and a sudden realization gripped her. She shivered though it wasn't cold. She instinctively knew what Janet was about to say.

"Mom," she gulped. "Mom," she repeated, slowly shaking her head back and forth. "Are you...do you..."

Janet nodded. "I believe," her voice was barely above a whisper. "I believe," she repeated, "that Taylor is Julie's baby boy." She dissolved into tears. Jennifer moved closer and put her arms around Janet and just held her while she cried.

When Janet had quieted down, Jennifer said softly, "Why? What makes you think so?"

"Pictures," she hesitated, "and memories. I dug out Julie and Brian's wedding album. On every page, Jennifer, it's Taylor looking at me through Brian's eyes, his appearance, even the way he holds his head. It's...it's uncanny."

Jennifer let out a long sigh. "Wow...wow." They sat in silence for another few minutes.

"Is there any chance it could be a huge coincidence?" Jennifer finally asked. "You have to admit it seems pretty bizarre."

"I suppose there's always a chance. But I have to say that if it is, it's mind boggling." She looked out the window and then back at Jennifer. "I guess we need to tell Tom. And I need to show you the photo album."

"Do you want to stay until he gets home from work? Oh, on second thought," Jennifer continued, "it would be better if we came over to your place unless you happened to bring the album with you?" she questioned. When Janet shook her head 'no', Jennifer decided, "I'll get a baby-sitter for tonight. OK?"

Janet nodded. "I think that would be good."

Being a do-it-now-don't-procrastinate kind of person, Jennifer jumped up and went for the phone. In less than three minutes, she had lined up a sitter for 7:30 that evening. "We'll be at your place about eight."

Janet left a bit later, drove straight home to get the album, then went on to Carmela's.

"You did the right thing," Carmela encouraged her after she related what happened at Jennifer's. "I had a feeling that would happen."

Carmela was leafing through the album for a second time. "Incredible," she remarked. "Looking at these photos, I don't see how it can be anybody *but* him." She closed the cover and set it down on the coffee table. "Do you have any idea where Brian is?"

"Not a clue," Janet replied. "I tried to stay in touch with him, sent him a few cards the first year or two after Julie died, but never got a response. Honestly, I don't even know if he's still alive."

"The other problem," Carmela noted, "is the Brodericks–the parents, I mean. It could be very traumatic for them as well as for Taylor."

"Believe me, I've thought of that," Janet agreed.

They talked a bit longer, creating various scenarios. As Janet prepared to leave for home, Carmela put her hands on Janet's shoulders, looked at her soberly and said, "Take it slow, my friend. Talk it over with your son. Taylor's not going anywhere. There's no need to rush. I'm confident you'll make the right decision in the end."

"Thanks, Carmela," Janet hugged her. "You're such a rock. Thanks."

Janet was just putting her supper dishes away when she heard Tom's voice call out from the front hall. "Hey, Mom. We're here." Janet emerged from the kitchen, dish towel in hand, smiled and said, "You're early. Did you have time to eat?"

"Picked something up on the way. We're fine. Jennifer wouldn't tell me what this was about–just that we needed to come over tonight. What's up?" Tom looked at his mother with obvious curiosity. "You know, I'm missing my favorite TV show to be here," he teased. Janet smiled at her handsome son.

Anticipating their arrival, Janet had the mugs out and ready for the hot chocolate, the trademark of Bradshaw gatherings, summer or winter. She still made it from scratch, like her mother and her grandmother before her. It was smooth, creamy and very chocolate-y, just the way they liked it.

She led Tom and Jennifer into the dining room where three photo albums were stacked in the middle of the table. Sitting down, she pulled the one on top towards her and looked soberly at her son. From across the table, Jennifer gave her an encouraging nod.

"Tom," she tilted her head towards him, "do you remember your Aunt Julie at all?"

"Not really, Mom. I was pretty young when she died, wasn't I?"

Janet nodded. "Two and a half," she said.

"Mostly I remember hearing you talk about her."

"Do you remember how she died, son?"

"Um...." Tom wrinkled his forehead. "Didn't she die having a baby?"

Janet was pleased that he remembered that much. She took up the narrative then, much as she had done with Carmela. Tom watched her closely as she reviewed the details of what had happened to the aunt he never knew. Janet noted the quizzical look on his face and knew he was trying to figure out where she was going with the story.

"What every happened to Brian?" he interrupted at one point.

"I don't know, son," she replied. "I don't even know if he's still alive."

"Did you ever find out what happened to the baby?" Tom pressed her. "I can't imagine any Dad doing that," he added, his face sober and sad.

Janet looked at Jennifer and then back at Tom.

Hardly above a whisper, she reached over and touched her son's hand, "That's why you're here."

Tom jerked his head up, surprise etched on his features. "What are you talking about?"

Janet opened the photo album to the first page and slid it across the table to Tom.

"That's your aunt and uncle on their wedding day." She watched him closely as he stared long and hard at the photo. He looked up at her, then turned his gaze back to the photo. He turned the page to look at the next photos. He turned another page and then another. Not a word. Jennifer was watching him, her eyes darting to Janet's from time to time.

He got to the last page then flipped the book back and stared again at the large photo on page one. Finally he looked up.

"Are there more pictures in those?" he asked, pointing to the additional two albums on the table.

Janet slid them over towards him. He looked through both albums, slowly, deliberately. When he finished, he leaned back in the chair and stared at nothing in particular.

After a few more moments of silence, Janet inhaled a deep breath. "I guess you see why I suspect that your friend, Taylor, may actually be your long lost cousin."

"Looks pretty convincing," he responded flatly. He stood up, ran his hands through his hair and walked over to the window, his back to his mother and his wife. Janet and Jennifer looked question-ingly at each other but said nothing.

Turning around he returned to the table. Jennifer was relieved to see that his face was calm. She detected no anxiety.

"What are you planning to do?" Tom addressed his mother.

"Nothing at the moment," she answered. "I've been wrestling with this for a couple of weeks already." She reached for the album and looked again at the wedding portrait. "There's a lot we don't know, Tom. For instance, if Taylor *is* who we suspect he is, how did he get from Toronto to England? More importantly, does he know he's adopted–if he is–and how does he feel about it? And his parents–they're getting up in years. I would never want to upset them–or him–or Catherine, for that matter.

"I don't know if we *ever* need to say anything. Maybe not. It could be that he never needs to know anything. Perhaps this is just God's way of letting me know that Julie's baby turned out just fine; that he's a lovely young man. I don't know, Tom," she concluded. "There's a lot to think about."

"I agree. I don't think we should say anything. First of all, they're new friends. We're just getting to know them. It would be highly inappropriate, I think, to say anything about this. Plus it could be really embarrassing if we turned out to be wrong.

There *is* a chance of that. People say that everybody has a twin somewhere in the world."

"You're right," Jennifer joined in. "My feeling is that we should just let this be. Put it on the proverbial shelf for now, let the friend-ship develop as it will. I'm a firm believer that if something is sup-posed to be, it will be. We don't have to force anything."

Janet smiled at her son and his wife. She was gratified at their attitude, proud of their maturity. They were right, of course. There was nothing to do at present.

On the drive home, Tom was uncharacteristically quiet. Jen-nifer let him be. About a block from their house, Tom gave a light chuckle. Jennifer reacted in surprise.

"I suppose stranger things have happened," he smiled, "but this sure is a doozie. If we ever find out that it's actually true, there ought to be a movie."

He chuckled again as he pulled in their driveway. "Looks like somebody's up past bedtime," he pointed to one of the second floor windows. A small face peered out through the curtain and the room went dark.

"Like father, like son," Jennifer quipped.

Chapter 15
Confrontations

In spite of herself, Paula Jean looked at the calendar and noted how many days were left until Ferko's return. Turning away quickly, she scolded herself. "Stop it," she said right out loud. "Stop it right now. Act your age, woman."

She pushed the mop a bit too aggressively across her kitchen floor. "This is absolutely ridiculous," she lectured herself. "Get a grip. You're going to end it once and for all and forget all about him. It's not right and you know it. Stop acting like a teenager, for heaven's sake."

Startled by the ringing of her phone, she ceased her scolding and answered sweetly, "Hello, I mean *Buon Giorno.*"

"It's just me, Cecilia," the British accent was unmistakeable. "You can forego the Italian. How are you?"

"Oh, fine, Cecilia, fine. How about you?"

"Lovely, thank you. I'm ringing you with some good news. My sister has decided to come for a visit. I'm quite excited about it, actually. I just got word this morning."

"Oh, that's very nice," Paula Jean responded, smiling to herself at the quaint expressions Cecilia used. "When is she coming?"

"A week from Tuesday. Her daughter is coming with her. Goodness, I haven't seen my niece in five or six years, maybe longer. Let me think. She's been working in America for at least five years. Before that, she interned in Ireland after graduating from university in Scotland. I saw her in Dublin when I was there on holiday about eight years ago. My, how time flies. She's a psychologist. Very bright young lady, I must say. I'm rather proud of her."

"I'm happy for you, Cecilia. How long will they be here?"

"I don't know, really," Cecilia laughed. "I didn't think to ask my sister when she called. Silly of me, wasn't it?

"You'll have to impress them with your new cuisine," Paula Jean declared.

"Oh, probably not," Cecilia laughed again. "They may disown me if they think I've lost my touch at making Yorkshire Pudding."

"I look forward to meeting them," Paula Jean remarked. "Have you told the others?"

"Carmela's not home and I haven't tried Janet yet. I'll call her next. Well, cheerio. See you tomorrow."

No sooner had she put the phone down when it rang again. "Sweet pea, how are you, my love?"

Her stomach recoiled into a tight knot at the sound of Ferko's voice. "I thought you weren't due back for a few more days?" she questioned.

"You're right, my darling. I'm still in...in Budapest but I just wanted to hear your voice." Paula Jean said nothing.

"Paula Jean? Are you still there?"

"Yes, I'm here," her voice was dull. "I'm...I'm just surprised to hear from you."

"I hope it's a good surprise, my love," he continued. "I can't wait to get back to you. Listen, I can't talk for long right now, but I'll see you in a few days, my darling." He clicked off.

Blast him, she thought as she slammed the phone down. She couldn't shake the sick feeling in the pit of her stomach every time she thought of him. *I wish I knew what it is*, she mused to herself. She returned to her house cleaning, venting her frustration with vigorous dusting and polishing of the furniture. If tables could talk, they would have cried out for mercy.

The next morning dawned bright and crisp. By mid-morning the Tuscan sun was high in the sky and the warmth of its rays were comforting to Paula Jean as she drove to Janet's for the women's weekly lunch. *I'm glad it's Janet's turn*, she thought to herself. I'd hate to be the first one to follow Cecilia's dinner the other night.

It was always comfortable at Janet's. No fine china to worry about, no delicate crystal goblets–just old fashioned glassware and sturdy Pfaltzgraff stoneware. Paula Jean rather liked Janet's dinnerware. It was called *Evening Sun* and Janet had purchased it just prior to moving to Italy. A colorful splash of sunflowers adorned the plates, bowls and mugs. It was the kind of table setting that made you smile whether you realized it or not. At least, it made a woman smile. Men don't notice such things, Carmela had insisted, at an earlier gathering at Janet's.

After a hearty lunch of baked Stuffed Shells, fresh vegetable salad and garlic bread, the women sat back to do what they did best–talk. "Isn't it amazing," Paula Jean had observed previously, "that no matter how often we get together, we always have plenty to talk about."

"Not amazing at all," Carmela shrugged her shoulders. "We're women. We talk. If there's nothing to say, we find something. It's who we are." There was hearty agreement around the circle.

"Great lunch, Janet," Carmela pronounced, as their hostess distributed dessert plates around the table.

"Thanks, glad you liked it," Janet smiled. She winked at Cecilia. "The bar has been set pretty high since Cecilia's dinner party."

"Oh, please don't feel that way," Cecilia protested.

"I don't," Janet answered. "Just felt a little more inspired this week." Cecilia grinned appreciatively.

"So...what's our next big adventure?" Carmela re-filled her glass with lemonade. "What's at the movies this week?"

"I haven't checked," Cecilia interjected, "but I do have some news. I didn't reach all of you by phone yesterday to tell you, but my sister is coming to visit. I just found out. She's bringing her daughter with her, too."

"That's great," Janet looked over at Cecilia. "How long since you've seen her?"

"About three years. And I haven't seen my niece in about five, maybe six years. She works in America–Chicago, I think. She's a psychiatrist."

"Oh no," Carmela acted horrified. "You mean I have to be good when they're around. I wouldn't want her to think you have a crazy friend." They all laughed.

"No worries," Cecilia protested. "I'm sure they'll both love all of you."

Janet brought out a scrumptious looking Lemon Meringue Pie and a pot of Jasmine Tea. Conversation ceased as they savored the creamy dessert and sipped their tea. After the dessert plates were cleared and the women were lingering over second cups of tea, Paula Jean squirmed in her seat and cleared her throat. Looking first at Carmela, her eyes went from one to the other, who were now all gazing at her expectantly.

"I want to bring something up," she said. "It's about Ferko...and me."

Janet and Cecilia looked at each other. Carmela kept her eyes on Paula Jean.

"As you know, he's been in Budapest and is due back here in a couple of days. While he's been gone, I've made a decision. I'm going to break off the relationship."

Carmela's expressions didn't change. Janet and Cecilia registered surprise.

"Why?" asked Cecilia. "if you don't mind my asking."

"Not at all," Paula Jean returned. "I've been feeling uncomfortable for some time and I wasn't actually sure why. At first I thought it was just a reaction to his showing up after so many years. I was shocked, frankly, and his behavior, his conversations with me at first seemed to indicate something–how should I say it–real? Something perhaps substantial?" She paused, groping for the right words.

"He asked me to marry him. I certainly wasn't ready for that so I said, 'no'. He kept at it and I started resenting the pressure he was putting on me. I think that was my first clue.

" I don't need to bore you with all the details but I just want to let you all know my decision. When he returns, I'm going to tell him and put this experience behind me. Since I've settled it, I feel so much better. I didn't realize how much it was weighing on me. I feel as though a heavy weight has lifted and I'm relieved.

Paula Jean took a deep breath, "I have to admit that I'm not looking forward to the confrontation. I've never liked confrontations. But the alternative is far worse so the sooner it's over, the better."

"I, for one, am proud of you, girlfriend," Janet spoke up. "For what it's worth, in the beginning I thought you and Ferko should get married. It seemed like such a fairy tale situation, but after awhile I think all of us could tell you weren't really happy." Her face brightened into a broad smile. "You're looking more relaxed. I'm glad. Besides, we've got a whole lot more adventures to experience together, the four of us. What do you say?" she finished, looking around the group.

"Absolutely," Carmela raised her tea mug in a mock toast. "Up with the Tuscany Golden Girls. Hear, hear!" They all raised their mugs with good-natured laughter.

"Well, I suppose all the truth should be told," Cecilia added. "I did *not* think you should get married and I said so to Carmela and Janet."

Carmela started to giggle. "Want to know what she really said?" Janet was also giggling now.

"What?" Paula Jean smiled dubiously.

"Oh, please...don't," protested Cecilia.

"She said Ferko might have hair in his ears and that was just not romantic!" Carmela exploded into laughter. The others joined in, including Paula Jean who laughed until tears were streaming down her face.

When they had quieted down, Paula Jean looked at Cecilia, opened her mouth to say something, then dissolved in laughter again. She finally composed herself and said, "That's very funny in itself. But it's even funnier coming from you, Cecilia. You're always so proper. I think it's hilarious that you were the one who said that."

"In self defense, let me also tell you the rest of what I said which I still think made perfect sense. I said that fifty years was a very long time and people change. You have no earthly idea what he's been doing all those years and neither does he know who you have become. I also said that you have a great life now and how horrible would it be if you ended up being an unpaid private nurse for a disabled old man, instead of enjoying the life you have at present."

"Sensible perspective. Just what I would expect from you, Cecilia. I will say, however, that even though I have a great life right now—and I love my life—if things had turned out differently with Ferko, if a real and deep love had in fact developed between us, I might have been willing to take that risk. But that's not what happened," she concluded. She looked at Carmela and smiled.

"Since we're sharing our viewpoints, I might as well add mine," Carmela leaned forward. "In the very beginning, I was all for the romance and the adventure. You all know that. But before long, I began to feel very uneasy about Ferko. I don't know why and don't want to know. It's not my business, but I support Paula Jean's decision. I think it's the right one and it's brought her peace of mind. That's important."

"Thank you all," Paula Jean looked gratefully at her circle of friends. "I can't tell you how much I appreciate each one of you."

"So...now that we've resolved that issue, who's going to check on what's playing at the movie theatre?" Carmela said jovially. "It's time for another trip to the movies."

"I second that," Paula Jean intoned.

"Me, three," Janet and Cecilia echoed at the same time.

The teapot had been re-filled and emptied four times over before the women finally left Janet's to return to their own homes. As Paula Jean climbed into bed a few hours later, she breathed a simple prayer of thanks for good friends and for peace of mind. She also asked for guidance in the upcoming confrontation.

At the same time Carmela was watching the late night news but her thoughts were elsewhere. The image of Ferko walking down a Paris street with another woman on his arm refused to leave her mind.

I hope I never have to tell her, she thought. *She doesn't need to know.*

Chapter 16
Family Connections

Cecilia's only sister, Eleanor, was born when Cecilia was ten years old and consequently the two girls were not close growing up. As an infant and toddler, Eleanor was more of a plaything than a sibling to the adolescent Cecilia and by the time teenage life with all of its activities was in full swing, Eleanor was more of a bother than a blessing to her older sister. What sixteen year old girl with a crush on the neighborhood soccer player wants her six year old sister following her around?

The passing of years didn't help. Cecilia married young and moved from her native London to Yorkshire where her husband was a medical student at the University of Leeds. Though the marriage only lasted four years, by the time they divorced, Cecilia was well established in her position as secretary to the Dean of the School of Education at the university. Therefore she stayed on in Leeds for several more years. Meanwhile, Eleanor navigated the challenges and charms of childhood and youth without the benefit of an older sister's watchful oversight. They were virtual strangers by the time Eleanor was eighteen.

The birth of Eleanor's daughter, Stephanie, in October of 1982 initiated the now warm relationship between Cecilia and her sister. Having no children of her own, Cecilia was quite excited about the baby and within months of Stephanie's birth, she resigned her position in Leeds and moved back to London in the spring of 1983. With an impressive CV and a superb letter of recommendation from her former superior, she was hired as executive assistant to the Director of Studies at the newly established Ashbourne College in Kensington where she continued working for many years. Cecilia thoroughly enjoyed the academic environment but nothing equaled the pleasure of spending time with her adorable niece.

Having grown up as if she were an only child, Eleanor reveled in the newfound relationship with her older sister. They spent a great deal of time together as both of them sought to recapture lost years of intimacy. Eleanor's husband, Harold, eight years older than his wife, was a typical English gentleman, deeply devoted to his wife and daughter. He was delighted, especially for Eleanor's sake, when Cecilia moved closer to them and he included her graciously in their family life and activities.

Stephanie had just celebrated her fourteenth birthday when Harold was tragically killed in an auto accident on the M1. He was returning from a business conference in Leeds and was a mere 10 miles outside of London when a car in front of him suddenly spun out of control and slammed into his BMW, crushing him in a monstrous tangle of hideously twisted metal and shattered glass.

A devastated Eleanor managed to summon impressive strength from within to support and comfort her daughter who had idolized her father. Cecilia grieved for her sister and her niece, but also for herself. She lost a dependable and very dear friend when Harold was taken from them.

The days immediately following the accident passed in a foggy blur of grief and sorrow interspersed with flashes of necessity as details were finalized for the funeral and legal documents were extricated from forgotten files far sooner than they should have been. Harold was not yet 50 when he died. Not only his family, but the business community as well, struggled to cope with the untimely loss of a respected corporate leader. Splattering raindrops turned into heavy showers the morning of his funeral as if the heavens rushed to join the long procession of mourners who came to pay their respects.

Over the new few weeks and months, Eleanor mourned her husband with dignity and courage, embracing the pain of her widowhood without self-pity or resentment. There was an inner strength about her that Cecilia had never witnessed before and she was in awe of Eleanor's selflessness. Stephanie, though heartsick with grief and so young besides, nevertheless mirrored her mother's serenity.

Cecilia alluded to it one day when her employer kindly inquired as to how her sister was adjusting. In response, he tilted his head and remarked, *Great souls are exposed when great tragedy calls them out of hiding.* Cecilia wrote the words in her notebook and reviewed them frequently. The concept moved her.

She'd had little to no religious upbringing and through the years had explored different approaches to spirituality, but never aligned herself with any particular religious system. For years she vacillated between faith and doubt, particularly after the keen disappointment of her failed marriage.

Eleanor's rock solid conviction that there is a God in the heavens Who loves His creatures and cares for them was difficult for Cecilia to share. Before Harold's death, Eleanor had the perfect life from Cecilia's viewpoint. A genteel husband who doted on her and provided generously, a beautiful and intelligent daughter, a respectable home in a lovely London neighborhood–all the things Cecilia did not have. She was never jealous but she was at times weary of coming home night after night to an empty apartment and she wondered how Eleanor could be so strong in the face of her loss.

About four months after Harold's death, Cecilia was having tea with Eleanor on a quiet Sunday afternoon. The conversation turned to spiritual matters as Eleanor showed her sister a book she was reading, *Entering the Castle.* Cecilia took it from Eleanor and perused the cover. Noting the subtitle, *Finding the Inner Path to God and Your Soul's Purpose*, she wrinkled her nose and opened to the Table of Contents. As she scanned the list, one particular section title stood out. It read *"The Second Mansion: God in the Details."*

She put the book down on her lap and looked over at Eleanor. "How far into the book are you?" she asked.

"More than half," Eleanor replied. "It's a very powerful read, Cecilia. I think you might like it."

"I don't know," Cecilia said slowly. She looked back at the Table of Contents until her eye fell again on the section title that had grabbed her attention. She read it aloud. "Do you really believe that?" she inquired of her sister.

"Believe what?"

"God in the details?" Cecilia shrugged. "That's a bit of a stretch for me."

Eleanor didn't say anything right away. She sipped her tea and took a bite of the scone while Cecilia withdrew into her own thoughts.

After a few quiet minutes, Eleanor asked, "Why?"

"Why what?" Cecilia blinked, then sipped her tea.

"Why is it such a stretch in your mind to believe that God could be involved in the details of our lives?"

Surprised at the question, Cecilia helped herself to a bite of scone, a deep frown creasing her forehead.

"I guess that means you do believe that," she finally responded, peering at Eleanor over the rim of her tea cup.

"You didn't answer my question," Eleanor smiled.

"Guess I didn't," Cecilia smiled back. "Well, for one thing, we weren't brought up to believe that. Mum and Father never talked about God or religion, did they?"

"No, they didn't. But haven't you ever been curious?"

"A little. I've read some books over the years but I didn't connect with them. I think I've rather dismissed people that focus on spirituality as kind of 'out there', you know. What they describe seems a bit unreal to me, I suppose."

Eleanor leaned forward slightly and looked intently into her sister's eyes. "I used to think the same way, Cecilia, until I married Harold. He's the one who introduced me to God." Eleanor searched her sister's face for a reaction. Cecilia's expression registered shock. "Really?" was all she could say.

"He wasn't a particularly religious man in the external sense," she continued, "but he had a vibrant faith. Actually, Harold was half Jewish. I don't think you ever knew that, did you?" Cecilia shook her head.

"His mother was Jewish but his father wasn't. Harold's mother was an amazing woman, Cecilia. I wish you could have known her. I'd never met anyone quite like her and I haven't since. Like Harold, she wasn't caught up in the outward expressions of her faith, though she did hold certain traditions very sacred and she kept them... faithfully." She paused.

" But, Cecilia, the woman had such faith in God. I learned so much from her....and from my husband who also learned it from her.

I'm not sure how to put it into words, but all I can tell you is that God was so real to both of them, it was as if He lived next door. Over time, He became real to me as well. Where do you think I've found the strength to carry on?" she raised her eyebrows as she gazed at Cecilia.

"I...you have a lot of inner strength..." Cecilia mumbled.

"But where does it come from?" Eleanor pressed her.

Cecilia closed her eyes and said nothing for a long time. When she opened them again, she said sadly, "I wish I could believe like you."

"You can, Cecilia. You can."

Cecilia looked away. Suddenly she felt as though a Stranger had just come between them. Their warm and close relationship felt abruptly fractured, fragile and insecure. A cold shiver slithered down her spine.

Eleanor sensed her sister's discomfort and never brought up the topic again.

All those memories and more were parading through her mind, as Cecilia made up the twin beds in her guest room in anticipation of Eleanor and Stephanie's arrival. She thought nostalgically of the pleasant memories, her cozy apartment in London, the fun times when Harold took them all to England's southern coast each summer. Her face clouded over and she felt a pang of sorrow as less pleasant memories pushed the early ones away.

She fluffed the pillows, opened the window to let in fresh air and after a final inspection of the room, breathed a simple prayer. "Oh God, if You can really hear me, please make this visit a good one."

Janet arrived five minutes later. Her roomy Toyota SUV was better suited for picking up family or friends at the airport than Cecilia's compact Fiat so Janet was typically the designated driver when any of the four women had visitors arriving from abroad.

Chapter 17
Shocked at the Airport

The flight was delayed. Cecilia groaned when she saw the announcement flashing on the Arrivals board.

"Where are you seeing that?" Janet frowned. "I don't even see a flight listed from London."

"Oh, they're not coming in from London. Eleanor took Stephanie to Paris for a couple of days before coming here. They're on that Air France flight, see it?" Cecilia pointed towards the marquis. "Let's get some coffee," she suggested. "Looks like we have at least an hour's wait."

The two women made themselves comfortable in a corner of A-Café and settled down to wait. Cecilia looked around the refurbished airport and declared the improvements 'lovely'. Located just three miles northwest of central Florence, Aeroporto di Firenze was smaller but much closer to the city than Pisa International Airport (Galileo Galilei), the arrival destination of most overseas tourists. For flights originating in Europe, however, the less trafficked AdF was the airport of choice. Its recent renovations had greatly improved its level of service. Several major European airlines such as Air France, Lufthansa, Swiss Air and KLM now offered direct flights to Florence from Paris, Munich, Brussels and other hubs on the continent.

Janet pulled a book from her purse and delved right into it while Cecilia flipped open a women's magazine left on a chair nearby by a previous patron. A newly installed flat screen TV was positioned on the wall opposite the table where Janet and Cecilia were sitting but neither of them paid it any attention.

About twenty minutes later they'd drained their coffee cups and Cecilia was getting restless. She nudged Janet to get her attention and said she was going to do a walkabout and would be back in a few minutes. Janet just smiled 'OK' and went right back to her book. *Must be a really good book*, Cecilia smiled to herself as she strolled away.

Having inspected the few shops in the terminal and purchased a copy of a UK magazine, *Woman and Home* that featured a smiling Helen Mirren on the cover, Cecilia made her way back to the café. She glanced casually at the television on the wall, noting that the streaming news feed was a BBC program. A distinguished looking reporter was speaking into the camera, obviously in an airport setting.

Janet looked up and smiled as Cecilia took her seat. "Nice walk?" she asked.

"It was good to move around a bit. It's pretty small as airports go, but there are a couple of interesting shops," Cecilia noted. She gestured with her head towards the television and said, "Look at that reporter. You never would have seen that when I was growing up in England. Times have changed, for the better, I must say."

Janet turned and reacted with a 'Wow, beautiful isn't she?'

"She really is," Cecilia agreed as both of them gazed at the reporter who spoke beautiful English with an impeccable British lilt. She was dressed in a tailored beige suit, her hair perfectly framing her delicately featured face. Though she exuded professionalism, her eyes sparkled with vitality which endowed her with a type of charisma. She was utterly charming in her seriousness. She was young and she was black.

The two women continued to watch the screen. Turning to her left, the reporter told the viewers, "This is Captain Villot of the Paris police."

"What can you tell us about the arrest made here at Charles De-Gaulle Airport a short time ago?" she asked the white haired officer.

"We are happy to announce that we have apprehended today someone we have been seeking for sometime," he said with a heavy French accent. "We caught him as he was preparing to leave the country. Some of the details are not, shall we say, ready to be told to the public until we do more investigation, but all I can tell you now is that it was very important for us to find him and stop his activities so we are very happy. Thank you very much." He walked away quickly.

Turning back to the camera, the winsome reporter concluded, "That is all we know at the moment but this man—a photo popped up on the screen to her right–was taken away in handcuffs by Paris police less than an hour ago. His name has not been released, nor do we know his alleged crime. We will bring you updated information as we receive it." The screen faded to a studio setting.

Janet and Cecilia never heard the last words of the reporter. Janet's face had blanched and was staring at the television with her mouth open. Cecilia was mindlessly repeating, 'Oh my God....oh my God....' The somber face on the televised police mug shot was unmistakeably the man they knew as Ferko.

Janet slid around in her chair, her face contorted in shock and disbelief. Cecilia didn't look any better. A man at the next table leaned over and said, "Are you ladies all right?"

His question snapped Cecilia out of her astonishment. She nodded, "Uh, thank you. Yes, we're OK." He looked doubtful but after hesitating briefly, turned back to his coffee and newspaper.

"Let's walk," Janet ordered, stuffing the novel into her purse. She got up quickly, took Cecilia's arm and said, "Come on."

They huddled together at the far end of the arrivals area in a fairly deserted corner. "I don't know what to think," Janet blurted out. "It's Ferko–it's him. But what..." she ran out of words.

"Indeed," Cecilia remarked. "What a shock!" She shook her head as if trying to eject the memory of what she'd seen. Suddenly she looked at Janet, "Wait a moment! Isn't he in Budapest? That was Paris. It can't be him. Maybe he has a twin or it's some horrible coincidence of someone who happens to look very much like him?"

"I don't know," Janet answered thoughtfully. "It would have to be an absolutely identical twin. Paula Jean never mentioned him having a brother. I can't imagine she wouldn't have known if he had a twin, especially one *that* identical!"

"Well, I just can't believe it's him. There has to be some mistake, some....something. It's just too terrible to even think about," Cecilia decided.

The loudspeaker announced the arrival of two flights, Air Berlin from Munich and Air France from Paris.

"Ah," Cecilia brightened up. "That's Eleanor's flight. Come on."

They hurried back the way they'd come, passed the Café and edged their way into the group of people, milling about as they waited for friends and loved ones. It didn't take long for Eleanor and Stephanie to come through the exit. They broke into huge smiles when they spotted Cecilia. Stephanie hurried her step, approaching her aunt with her arms spread wide. She grabbed Cecilia and twirled her around, squealing, "It's *so* good to see you!" Eleanor followed her daughter's lead and embraced her sister warmly, kissing her on both cheeks.

Cecilia introduced Janet then and Stephanie hugged her as well. "So pleased to meet you," she smiled. Eleanor was less demonstrative but still very warm and personable.

"Have you been waiting long?" Eleanor turned back to Cecilia. "It was a bit eventful at the other end."

"What happened?" Janet asked.

"We were on board already," Stephanie interjected, "and as the last few passengers took their seats, suddenly six heavily armed gendarmes burst onto the plane, grabbed a passenger seated a few rows ahead of us and dragged him off the plane. It was surreal."

"Yes," Eleanor picked up the story, "and there was an older woman across the aisle from us who didn't understand what was happening and started screaming, 'Hijack, Hijack'. It took the flight attendant quite some time to calm her down and assure her that we were not hijacked. The poor woman was terrified."

Cecilia gave Janet a sideways glance then quickly changed the subject. "The important thing is that you're here now. Let's get going. We're going to have a lovely time."

Eleanor and Stephanie kept up a lively conversation with Cecilia all the way home so no one paid much attention to the fact that Janet was extremely quiet. The image on the television screen haunted her thoughts as she drove. What in the world were they going to do? How would Paula Jean take the news? Did she already know? If not, should they tell her? But what if it really wasn't Ferko?

Then again, Paula Jean had already decided to end the relationship, so would it be so terrible after all when she learned the truth about him?

When they arrived at Cecilia's, Janet declined an invitation to stay for supper. "You three have plenty to talk about, I'm sure, and we'll see lots of each other during the next two weeks," she smiled as she waved good-bye to Cecilia, Eleanor and Stephanie. "Lunch at my place next week, don't forget!" she called back as she drove away.

Instead of going straight home, Janet detoured to Carmela's. Relieved to see the car in the driveway, she pulled in behind the Volvo and made a dash for Carmela's front door.

In less time than it took to heat the water for tea, Janet related to Carmela what she and Cecilia had witnessed at the airport. Carmela was uncharacteristically quiet and non-responsive.

"Hey, what gives?" Janet asked. "I just tell you this bombshell and you have no reaction?"

Carmela gave a sad smile as she carried two cups of tea to the kitchen table.

She sat down opposite Janet, looked directly at her and said simply, "I'm not surprised."

"What?!" Janet was incredulous.

Soberly, Carmela told Janet about the late afternoon news broadcast she'd seen a few weeks earlier. She'd known since then that Ferko was not in Budapest but in Paris and what she'd seen had only confirmed the sense of distrust and uneasiness she'd had about him for a long time.

"So he has another woman in Paris," Janet stated flatly.

"I don't know," Carmela answered. "I suppose it could be an older sister or a relative. I didn't see her face, and I've tried not to assume anything, but considering what you saw today, there's one thing for sure. Paula Jean is absolutely right to break off any ties with him."

"Hmm," Janet remarked, "she may not ever have to confront him. Right now, he's in police custody in Paris." She stared out the window for a few moments. "Don't you wonder what in the world he was doing to bring on the arrest?"

Carmela shrugged her shoulders. "Oh, I don't know. I'm more concerned about Paula Jean than Ferko. If he's guilty of some crime, he'll get his due. But Paula Jean... even though she's already decided to break it off, it's not going to be easy for her to find out he's accused of some crime. Nobody wants to feel like they've been duped by a criminal, or anyone else, for that matter, even if the relationship is over."

"You're right," Janet gave a little laugh. "When I was a teenager, I had a crush on one of the football players in our high school and I flirted with him shamelessly."

She rolled her eyes. "After a couple of weeks I found out he had a steady girlfriend. First I felt like an idiot; then I got mad that he never discouraged my flirting. I was mad, mostly at myself."

"So–what do you think we should do?" Carmela raised an eyebrow. "Do we tell her before she hears it on TV?"

Janet leaned forward, resting her chin on her hands, and stared into her empty tea cup, thinking.

"If it were me, I would be very upset to find out that my best friends knew what was going on, and they didn't tell me," Carmela remarked. "Besides, I think it would be cruel of us to let her find out about it like you did–on the television–or in a newspaper article. That's how I would feel–betrayed, let down by my friends."

"Besides," Carmela continued, "she thinks Ferko is due back here in a day or two and she's getting all worked up about the confrontation–for nothing. He's not coming back. She needs to know that."

"You're right," Janet nodded, then added, "Cecilia should be in on the conversation, but with her sister here...."

"Not a problem," Carmela always knew how to figure things out. "I'll give Cecilia a call and we'll arrange an appropriate time that won't interfere with her sister or niece."

"OK," Janet agreed. "The sooner, the better."

Carmela dialed the number and Cecilia picked up on the first ring.

"How is your sister?" Carmela began. "I'm really happy for you that she and her daughter came to visit."

"Oh, it's great, Carmela. They just got here a couple of hours ago but we haven't stopped talking yet. I'm looking forward to you meeting them."

"Me, too," Carmela answered. "Meanwhile, Janet's told me about what you and she saw on the television at the airport. What you didn't know is that I had previously seen Ferko on a television broadcast from Paris a couple of weeks ago.

Long story short, we need to meet as soon as possible. I think we need to talk to Paula Jean. I told Janet that if it were me, I'd be devastated if my friends knew something like this and didn't tell me. What do you think?"

Cecilia was quiet for a few moments and then said, "I think you're right. It won't be easy but I think we need to do it and probably, the sooner the better."

"That's what Janet said, too. Do you think you could spare an hour or so tomorrow without interfering with your sister and niece?" Carmela asked.

"Don't you worry, I'll take care of it. Where are we meeting and when?" Cecilia answered.

"How about my house? Ten o'clock?" Carmela suggested.

"I'll be there," Cecilia clicked off.

Chapter 18
Hidden Things Come to Light

Paula Jean was up early and by eight am had already weeded a large portion of her garden. It was a beautiful morning and she loved being outdoors at this time of day when everything was new and fresh after the nighttime dew. Deciding it was time for her coffee, she was picking up her garden tools when she heard the phone ringing. She made her way quickly through the back entryway, dropped her garden tools into the metal bucket by the door and stepped into the sunlit kitchen. Lifting the phone from its cradle, she said a crisp, *"Buon Guorno."*

A heavily accented male voice asked if she was Mrs. Paula Jean Jackson. The man's tone alarmed her. "Who is this?" she inquired coldly.

"Mi Scusi, Signora, I am calling from the *Questura* (Florence Police Headquarters). *Per favore,* can you tell me–do you know someone by name of Ferko Molnar?"

Paula Jean froze. "Has something happened to him?" she asked.

"So you know him, *Signora?"*

"Well, yes. Has something happened to him?" Paula Jean asked again.

"No, no. *Grazie. Ciao."* The line went dead.

The familiar knot in her stomach returned. How strange, she thought, as her feelings of distrust re-surfaced. She hardly had time to think any further when the phone rang again.

"Yes," she answered abruptly.

"Paula Jean, are you all right?" It was Carmela.

"Oh, sorry," she breathed heavily into the phone. "I just had the strangest phone call from the Florence Police and I thought it was them calling back."

"Are you OK?" Carmela repeated. "Is something wrong?"

"No, no, I'm fine. It was so bizarre, Carmela. They wanted to know if I knew Ferko. After I said 'yes', they just thanked me and hung up. It was really weird."

Carmela swallowed hard, then continued, "Paula Jean, can you come over about ten this morning? The four of us need to get together, We've got something to talk about."

"Uh, sure, OK," Paula Jean was taken aback. "Anything you can tell me now?"

"Just come on over. I've already called the others."

"Ok, then. See you in a little while." Paula Jean put the phone down, made her way down the hall to her bedroom, all the while thinking this was a very strange morning indeed.

Promptly at ten, Cecilia pulled up in front of Carmela's house with Paula Jean right behind her. Janet was already there. There was freshly baked banana bread on the kitchen island, along with coffee mugs, a sugar bowl and creamer. Paula Jean noticed two bottles of wine with four wine glasses on the counter opposite. *Strange*, she thought, *for so early in the day*. But she made no comment aloud.

With no preamble, Carmela plunged right in. "I called this meeting because something very important has come up and we need to talk about it." She gestured toward the patio as she said, "Get yourselves some coffee and banana bread and let's go out back." She had previously arranged four chairs in a circle around a low patio table covered with a red and white checkered tablecloth.

"I'll get right to the point," Carmela continued when all the women were seated. "I hate beating around the bush." Looking directly at Paula Jean, she said, "The three of us have something to share with you that will confirm your decision to break off with Ferko. And you know you have our full support in that."

Paula Jean was completely perplexed. She looked around the circle, sensing that something was coming.

"Janet, will you tell Paula Jean what you saw at the airport yesterday?"

Janet nodded and gently described to Paula Jean the television broadcast announcing Ferko's arrest in Paris. Cecilia added that she, too, had witnessed it.

"Paris?" Paula Jean looked confused. "But I thought...." Her voice trailed off.

"We *all* thought he was in Budapest," Carmela continued. "At least I did, until the day of Cecilia's dinner party."

Paula Jean's eyes widened as she cocked her head. "What do you mean?"

"I turned my television on that day when we all went home to change, and I happened to see a BBC broadcast from Paris. I knew it was Paris because the Eiffel Tower was in the background. I saw Ferko walking down the sidewalk behind the reporter with–with an older woman on his arm." Carmela paused. "I was stunned, What was he doing in Paris? Then I thought that maybe I was mistaken and tried to put it out of my mind."

"But yesterday," Cecilia spoke up, "when Janet and I were at the airport waiting for my sister, we saw the broadcast Janet told you about. I'm so sorry, Paula Jean, but there is no doubt it was Ferko. He was taken off my sister's plane by the French police but we don't know what he's alleged to have done. We just didn't want you to hear about it from someone else. And we didn't want you to stress over the confrontation you were planning to have with him, when we knew he wasn't coming back." She paused, "I hope you're not upset with us."

Paula Jean closed her eyes, then exhaled deeply. Those gut feelings of distrust, the annoyance at his secretive ways, the mood swings she'd observed–it all came back to her in waves of stark reality. There *was* something very wrong. Her intuition had not been mistaken.

Opening her eyes, she looked at her friends and sensing their apprehension, she said, "Thank you—thank you so much for telling me. I don't know what I really feel right now except that you're right, I'd much rather hear this from my best friends than from a news program," she paused, "or the Florence Police!"

The others relaxed as Paula Jean continued, "Wow–I'm glad I had already made the decision to break off my relationship with him.

You were right, Cecilia. Fifty years is a long time and I *didn't* know what he'd been doing all those years. He never wanted to talk about it. Obviously, there was a reason."

Suddenly she bolted straight up, "Oh goodness, whatever he's done, I hope the Florence Police don't think I'm in on it!"

"I doubt that," Janet said, "but don't worry, we've got a great lawyer in the family," she grinned.

"Gee, thanks," Paula Jean groaned.

"Seriously," Carmela interjected, "I don't think you have anything to worry about. Just thank God you were smart enough to see through him."

"I didn't at first," Paula Jean replied, feeling a little embarrassed.

"But it didn't take long for you to catch on," Carmela remarked. "We're not grey haired for no reason. We've learned a few things over the years. All of us have."

The four women talked a bit longer, relishing the very special friendship they enjoyed. No one had to comment on it; they all felt it. And they were all deeply thankful.

Half an hour later, Paula Jean suddenly gave a little giggle. "This is crazy. I was dreading the confrontation with Ferko and I stressed over it for nothing. I don't even have to see him again." She laughed out loud. "I actually feel relieved."

Turning to Carmela, she quipped, "By the way, I saw wine on the counter in there. Unusual for this early in the morning?"

With a grin, Carmela replied, "I didn't know exactly how this was going to go so I figured I needed to have some wine handy, just in case we needed it for tension relief. I should have known better!"

"Bring it on," Janet declared. "This is as good a reason as any to toast our friendship–again."

ৡৡ

During the following weeks, more and more details slowly emerged regarding Ferko Molnar's crimes. When Paula Jean learned that he had a wife–of thirty-eight years no less–living in Paris, and two grown sons, she was livid. "That scoundrel!" she exploded to Janet and Cecilia. "How dare he wine and dine me!"

A few days later when the full scope of the fraud he had perpetrated against naïve widows across Europe hit the newspapers, Paula Jean as well as the other three women were shocked, dismayed and angry all at the same time. They wre particularly upset when they learned that among the victims was a neighbor of Janet's, an octogenarian whom Janet described as "one of the sweetest women you could ever meet."

The Florence police called Paula Jean again to inform her that her bank account numbers had been found among Ferko's papers and their investigation had confirmed that he had hacked into her accounts on his laptop. They recommended she confer with her personal banker to create new accounts for her since one of Ferko's accomplices was still at large.

The other three women did the same. No one was taking any chances for after all, they fit the profile of the kind of women Ferko had systematically victimized over the past three years.

The media had its heyday with the crime and public disgust accelerated the prosecution. In less than three months, Ferko was sentenced to prison for a very long time.

In the end, Marguerite was the most pitiful victim. Her hero was no hero at all, but a scoundrel, a criminal, a liar and a womanizer. She was devastated and humiliated beyond recovery. About two months after Ferko was sentenced to prison, Carmela happened to see a small article in the Italian newspaper, reporting the suicide death of Marguerite Molnar, wife of Ferko Molnar, the infamous fraud recently incarcerated. According to the article, Marguerite's sons buried her quietly in a small cemetery outside Paris, then quickly left the country of their birth, vowing never to return.

Chapter 19
New Beginnings

Six months later, Eleanor returned to Tuscany to be near her sister permanently. The earlier visit with her daughter, Stephanie, had exceeded her greatest expectations. She and Cecilia had been drawn together in those two weeks in a way that neither had anticipated. Stephanie, seeing her mother and aunt getting on so well together, had encouraged Eleanor to consider selling the family home in England and relocating to the warmer climate of Italy. England could be miserable in winter and with Stephanie living and working in New York, Eleanor had no reason to endure another British winter by herself in the large family home, Stephanie insisted.

So, shortly after returning from Florence, she'd retained the services of an estate agent. Not surprisingly, her lovely home sold in the first month. Eleanor wrapped up all her affairs, bid farewell to her lifelong friends, sorted through what she would move to Tuscany and what she would sell or give away, and in six short months, she became an expat among expats, happily settling into a lovely cottage not far from Cecilia's. The "Tuscany Golden Girls" had a new member.

Over coffee one morning as she was helping Eleanor decide where to hang artwork and family photos, Cecilia finally admitted to Eleanor that she had been very apprehensive before her sister's earlier visit.

"We hadn't been together for quite some time, really," Cecilia said, "and I wasn't terribly receptive to your spirituality, if you remember. I was afraid we would be miles apart in outlook and perhaps have too little in common."

Eleanor smiled, "It didn't turn out that way, did it?"

"Not at all. And I give you the credit for that. Honestly, I don't know if I will ever have a faith as strong as yours, but I so appreciate that you accept me just the way I am and I love you for that." She gave her sister a quick hug and added, "I'm so glad you're here. And by the way, so are the others. You fit right in with us."

"I loved your friends right away. They're such a special group of women. I told Stephanie that I felt like I was moving into an extended family. She agreed. By the way, what time do we have to leave for the Cafe?"

Cecilia glanced at her watch. "Oh my, it's nearly eleven-thirty. We should leave in about five minutes."

The two sisters put aside the rest of the photos for another day, freshened up and were soon enroute to Café Toscana for the regular bi-monthly lunch meeting that was part and parcel of the group's social life.

Janet and Cecilia were already there when they arrived. Carmela sauntered in about three minutes later with Paula Jean. The Café was crowded but the service never suffered. The waiters were outstanding, as always.

As per usual, the women ordered two main entrees, a large salad and generous basket of Italian bread with olive oil for dipping. Their waiter brought five plates and each woman served herself from the large platters. They had learned early on to forego individual orders as none of them could eat the generous portions. Sharing as they did was just right.

After their pasta and salad, the waiter knew what to do without a word from the ladies. Three large cannolis, artistically arranged on a rectangular serving plate, were drizzled with chocolate sauce and garnished with fresh strawberries. The colorful dessert plates were distributed, along with a steaming cappuccino for each of the ladies.

As they lingered over dessert and coffee, Janet mentioned in passing that Taylor's father was not well at all. The Parkinson's had progressed to the point that he could no longer be cared for at home. Taylor had flown to England, she added, to help his mother find a suitable nursing facility for his father and get him settled into it. Catherine had remarked to Jennifer that it was very difficult on Taylor to see his father so debilitated.

Later that same evening, Jennifer phoned Janet with the startling news that Taylor's father had very suddenly passed away a couple of hours earlier. No one expected it. His physician was as shocked as they were. The senior Mrs. Broderick was having a very difficult time coming to grips with her husband's sudden death. Jennifer had offered to keep the children so that Catherine could join Taylor in England for the funeral. After several phone calls back and forth, in the end Catherine decided to take the children with her. She hoped that it would be a comfort to her mother-in-law to have her grandchildren there.

Tom called Janet first thing the next morning to say that he was flying to England for the funeral and thought it would be nice if she would go with him. "Like representatives of Taylor and Catherine's 'Italian family', in a way," he said. Both of them realized it was actually more than that, but neither of them voiced the thought.

Janet pulled her overnight bag from her storage room, packed quickly and was ready when Tom pulled up an hour later. He had arranged for their tickets to be waiting for them at the check-in counter and in no time, they were airborne.

Taylor was visibly moved to see Tom and Janet show up at the funeral parlor, as was Catherine. The senior Mrs. Broderick was shrouded in grief and shock and hardly knew who was there, but did acknowledge their arrival with the saddest smile Janet had ever seen.

After the funeral service had ended, Tom and Janet spent a few hours back at the family home with Taylor, Catherine and Taylor's Mom before leaving for the airport and the flight back to Italy.

As they said their farewells, Catherine took Janet aside and with tears in her eyes, said, "You'll never know how much it meant to Taylor for you to come all the way from Italy–you and Tom. He has always wished he had a larger family—siblings, aunts, uncles, cousins—but he never did. It was just the three of them all his life. You and your family, as well as the other ladies, have become our family. You all mean so much to both of us." With tears spilling over, Catherine drew Janet into a warm and long embrace. "Thank you so much," she whispered.

It took every ounce of control that Janet could muster to maintain her composure. She was smiling at Catherine but inside she was thinking, *"Oh, if you only knew how much we **are** family...Maybe some-day..."*

Taylor and Catherine stayed on for another week to help Mrs. Broderick with paperwork and the multitude of details that accompany the passing of a loved one. She had aged considerably in the past few days and seemed so fragile. Half way through the week they convinced her to return with them to Italy for an undetermined amount of time while she adjusted to the reality of being a widow. She meekly agreed.

Near the end of the week, as Taylor was cleaning out his father's file cabinet, he stumbled across a folder labeled "Adoption Records". He laid it aside to look at later and continued emptying the drawer.

Catherine wandered into the room a few minutes later, noticed the file and picked it up. She leafed through the official documents that had made her husband the legal son of Philip and Bronwyn Broderick, reading through them for the first time. She had known that he was born in Toronto but never thought much about it. Now as she turned page after page, she was fascinated by details she had never known. Towards the back of the file, she found a copy of a death certificate for a Julie Butler, a handwritten letter signed by a Rosalie Hixson, authorized representative of the International Adoption Agency of Canada, and Taylor's original birth certificate, yellowed and faded. She started putting the information together and understood for the first time that Taylor's mother must have died the day he was born. She shivered at the realization, her mind imagining what horrific grief and despair must have overcome Taylor's real father—that is, if in fact, he was there for the birth.

She pressed on. The next page was a marriage certificate. *Aha, she thought, they were married, so he must have been there.* It was a copy, not the original, and some of the words were hard to read. She could make out 'Brian' but the last name was illegible except for the last letter which was an 'r'. Clearly the bride's first name had been Julie but someone had rubbed out her family name. The date of the marriage indicated that these must have been Taylor's birth parents. The timing was appropriate.

She was so engrossed in reading through the file that she failed to realize that Taylor had stopped what he was doing and was reading over her shoulder until she heard him gasp. She looked up quickly and saw his troubled expression.

"Honey, are you all right?" Catherine searched his face.

"Yeah," he nodded. "Just wasn't ready to see all that today."

"I'm sorry, darling," Catherine said, touching his arm. "I saw it on the table and just picked it up. I....there's a lot in here."

"I see that," Taylor replied. "Can we put it aside for another time?"

"Sure, honey, sure. I'm sorry," Catherine said as she slid all the papers back into the folder and closed the cover.

"I think we should take that with us," he said quietly, then turned back to sorting through more files.

Catherine took the Adoption Records file back to Taylor's old bedroom where they were staying and slipped it into her carry-on. She'd take good care of it for him until he was ready to pore over it.

Meanwhile, she was pleased to have the information available. Someday it could prove important.

Chapter 20
Closing the Gap

Bronwyn Broderick had been in Italy nearly six months and the longer she stayed, the less inclined she was to return to Essex. Her grandchildren did more for her than any grief therapy could have, and she felt safe in the home of her son and daughter-in-law. Taylor and Catherine had welcomed her to stay as long as she wished and were more than content to have her there. In large part, her extended stay was mutually comfortable because in so many ways, Catherine was the daughter Bronwyn had never had, but secretly longed for over the years. Their relationship was warm, honest and relaxed, a blessing neither of them took for granted.

She also found comfort in socializing with Carmela, Cecilia, Janet and Paula Jean, as well as the other newcomer, Eleanor. They were sensitive to her newly widowed state, but at the same time, gently drew her into their activities, helping her in subtle ways to begin to discover 'life after Philip'.

Meanwhile, Eleanor had become what Carmela called 'a real Tuscan'. She quickly learned a few words in Italian, easily mastered the art of navigating the open market, and tried her hand at gardening in a new climate with great success. Not for a moment did she ever regret making the move from England to Italy. She and Cecilia enjoyed the best relationship they'd ever had and Stephanie, when she visited her Mum's new home, had pronounced the move "the best thing Mum ever did, after marrying Daddy and having me, of course!"

As summer rolled around, Paula Jean enrolled in a summer course in landscape painting at the Florence Academy of Art. Janet and Carmela registered for a course in how to make stained glass, taught by a local artisan and Cecilia, now a *bona fide* 'foodie', signed up for a chef's class in one of Florence's best known cooking schools. Though Cecilia invited her along, Eleanor declined to join her sister, preferring instead to study Italian with a retired teacher who was her neighbor. Despite their active lives, the five women maintained their regular routine of weekly lunches, rotating from one home to the other and bi-monthly jaunts to Café Toscana for coffee and cannolis. Bronwyn had begun to join in during her fourth month in Italy.

Seeing the other five women involved in learning something new, Bronwyn surprised Catherine one morning by announcing that she'd like to learn a new skill as well, but first she needed to attend to unfinished business, like selling her home in England and moving permanently to Italy to be near Tom and Catherine.

"What do you think?" she asked her daughter-in-law.

Catherine was delighted and assured Bronwyn that Taylor would be as well, not to mention the grandchildren. "They'll be thrilled, Mom," Catherine hugged her.

"The children love having you here."

"I've been thinking about it for a few weeks. There's nothing left for me in England. You're the only family I have and with Taylor doing so well in his position and all of you so happy here, I don't foresee you moving back to England anytime soon."

Catherine laughed, "You've got that right. Who would want to trade the magnificent sunshine and beautiful surroundings we have for grey and gloomy England?"

"We do have some nice weather at times," Bronwyn answered defensively.

"I know, Mom, but seriously, compared to Tuscany?" Catherine raised an eyebrow.

Bronwyn smiled, "You win, of course."

When Taylor came home from work that evening, the three of them had a round table discussion about Bronwyn's projected plan. As Catherine had predicted, Taylor was more than pleased. As the only son, he had predictably assumed the protector's role towards his mother after his father's death.

The grandchildren squealed and hugged her when she told them her plans. Bronwyn beamed. It was the first really broad smile on his mother's face that Taylor had seen since his father passed away. He remarked later to Catherine, "I always thought Mum was content to be a homebody, but she's actually becoming quite social. I think it's great. Maybe Dad was the real homebody and held her back." Catherine nodded, "Maybe so."

The next day Catherine took Bronwyn to meet with the estate agent in Florence who had helped them find a house when they arrived in Italy. By late that afternoon, Bronwyn and Catherine had seen five available properties nearby and Bronwyn was quite sure which one she would choose but she wanted Taylor to check it out before she signed on the dotted line. It was a grey stucco two bedroom, two bath with a sloping roof of terracotta tiles, a cobbled front pathway and a moderately sized flower garden in back with a stately olive tree at the center. It also boasted a stone fireplace in the living room, which Bronwyn loved, a dining room that would comfortably accommodate her traditional English dining room furniture and an updated kitchen. There was a driveway to its left and best of all, Bronwyn thought, was its location. It was next door to Janet.

That evening they met the estate agent for a second look, this time with Taylor. Bronwyn had called Janet and asked her to join them as well. Then, deciding she didn't want to leave anyone out, she called all the others so when the estate agent arrived at seven o'clock, Carmela, Cecilia, Eleanor, Paula Jean, Janet, Tom and Jennifer, Taylor, Catherine and Bronwyn were all chatting away rather excitedly in the driveway.

With their unanimous approval behind her, Bronwyn signed the contract that evening to purchase the *casa*. Over the next few days, she and Catherine made a list of the furniture she had in England, decided what should be sold and what should be shipped to Florence, planned the re-decorating of the rooms, choosing paint colors and shopping for window treatments and other small items not worth shipping from Bronwyn's Essex home, and arranged for Bronwyn's trip back to England to put the property into the hands of an estate agent. Taylor took two weeks of comp time he'd accumulated to accompany his mother and help with arrangements.

While they were away, Carmela and Janet chose a final project for their 'test' at the end of the stained glass making course they were taking. They began work on a colorful insert for the front door of Bronwyn's new home. The result was exquisite.

Paula Jean had just completed a beautiful painting of the Tuscan countryside and decided it would be a fitting housewarming gift for Bronwyn.

Cecilia jumped at the opportunity to cater the Housewarming Party, putting her culinary skills to good use and sharing with her friends some of the great recipes she was learning in cooking school.

Eleanor wasn't quite sure what to do until Catherine mentioned one day that she was having difficulty finding the kind of curtains her mother-in-law wanted for the master bedroom. Immediately, Eleanor responded, "Tell me what she'd like and I'll make them for her. I love to sew and I have a great machine. I'd love to do it."

When Taylor and Bronwyn returned from England, everything was arranged and Bronwyn already had a solid offer on her former home. It was just a matter of time to closing. A mere six weeks later, Bronwyn moved into the grey stucco. Her furniture and goods from England had arrived two days earlier and with everyone's help the rooms were settled with relative ease and at the end of the day, only a few boxes remained to be unpacked.

The Housewarming Party was scheduled for the following Sunday, giving Eleanor enough time to finish the bedroom curtains. It had taken some time to locate just the right fabric and though Eleanor was an experienced seamstress, she was also a perfectionist and therefore, worked a bit more slowly than someone who just wanted to get the job done.

Cecilia recruited Carmela's help with the cooking and between them, they prepared a banquet "fit for the Queen", Bronwyn exclaimed, when she saw the sumptuous feast.

The stained glass piece was gorgeous and Taylor called his handyman on the spot, scheduling him to install it the next day. Paula Jean's painting would hang over the fireplace. Tom went looking for a hammer and nails and had it up before the party was over. Afterwards, he and Taylor hung the bedroom curtains and all the ladies took their turn checking out Eleanor's creation. As a result, Eleanor became the designated seamstress for the group from that day on.

The food leftovers were divided among the departing guests as Bronwyn protested that she couldn't possibly eat all that food herself. Generous portions were packed up for her grandchildren and an equally generous package went with Tom and Jennifer for their children. Janet was the only one who declined taking any food but said, "I'll just come over and eat with Bronwyn tomorrow. How's that for inviting myself?" she smiled.

Taylor and Catherine were the last to leave after the party. "Is there anything you need, Mum, before we go?" Taylor asked.

"Thank you, son. No, I'm fine. It was such a lovely party, wasn't it?" she replied.

"It really was," Catherine commented. "And the food....oh, my!" she continued. "I'll have to diet for the next couple of days to recover."

"Mum," Taylor put his hands on her shoulders, "I just want to tell you how happy I am that you're here and I'm really proud of how you're recovering from losing Dad. He'd be really proud of you, too."

Her eyes glistened as she looked up at her handsome son. "I love you, Taylor. Thank you for all your help." Turning towards Catherine, she added, "You, too, darling. I couldn't have done it without the two of you."

"Are you sure you'll be all right here by yourself?" Taylor's face took on a serious expression.

"Of course, I will. Now get along home and don't worry about me. I love my new little house and Janet is right next door. Go on, now. Drive carefully."

"Oh, Mum," Taylor chuckled. "You'll probably tell me to drive carefully until I'm fifty!"

"Longer than that, if I'm still alive," she quipped back, laughing, as Taylor and Catherine went out the door.

She watched until they pulled out of the driveway and took off down the street. From the side window in her living room, she could see that Janet's lights were still on. Bronwyn smiled to herself, a contented, peaceful smile. She turned and walked back to the bedroom. *I hope Taylor's right*, she mumbled softly, as she lifted her eyes to the ceiling. *I hope you're proud of me, Philip.*

Taylor was quiet most of the way home. As they turned off the highway toward their neighborhood, he said, "It's hard to process all that's happened in the past few months."

Sensing he wasn't finished, Catherine said nothing.

"I miss my Dad," he said matter-of-factly. "I still find myself thinking sometimes that it can't be real. I mean, he was always there."

"I miss him, too," Catherine whispered.

"I never thought Mum would move out of the house. We lived our whole lives there." He was quiet for a couple of minutes.

"I'm glad, though," he resumed. "I'm really glad now. It's better for all of us that she's here."

Catherine reached over and squeezed his hand. He turned toward her as they swung into their driveway. "Thank you," he said quietly.

"For what?" she looked curiously.

"For everything, that's what," he leaned over and kissed her cheek. "You rock, Lady Catherine!" he declared, smiling impishly at her. "What do you say we call it a night? Race you to the bedroom!" He bolted out of the car and ran, laughing, towards the front door, with Catherine chasing close behind.

Chapter 21
Neighbors

One morning a few weeks later, Janet was snipping roses from the potted plant by her front door when Bronwyn called over to her, "How about some coffee with your neighbor?"

"Be right over," she smiled back.

Janet slipped into her kitchen, put three of the roses in a small glass vase, washed her hands and took the other three roses she'd snipped over to Bronwyn. They were intensely yellow and were stunning in Bronwyn's cobalt blue glass vase. She promptly displayed them on her walnut coffee table. The roses added a finishing touch to an already lovely room.

Bronwyn's traditional English furniture stood out beautifully against the sun-washed walls of the living room. When she was planning her décor with Catherine, she had decided on a pale but sunny color for the living room as it had only three windows in the typical arched style of Tuscan homes. She wanted the room to be cheerful and bright and her color choice was a winner. The living room was warm and inviting, soft and light.

The kitchen, where she and Janet were enjoying their coffee and croissants, was more colorful, more Tuscan. The yellow was deeper, the red bolder and the cobalt blue glassware displayed on an open shelf was a decorating statement any interior designer worth her salt would have applauded. The living room may have been English, but the kitchen was definitely Tuscan.

The two women made themselves comfortable at the kitchen table. The aroma of freshly baked something had greeted Janet at the door and as she took a bite of the butter-pecan-oatmeal muffins, she closed her eyes and murmured her approval with an enthusiastic 'Mmmmmm.'

Bronwyn grinned, "Pretty good, aren't they?"

"I'll say," Janet acknowledged. "Is this one of those secret family recipes or can I beg a copy?"

Bronwyn laughed. "No secret here," she countered. "It's right out of my *Woman & Home* magazine. I'll get you something to write with and you can copy it now, if you'd like."

"Great, thanks," Janet replied, taking another bite of her muffin. "These are scrumptious."

In the course of their casual conversation, Bronwyn mentioned in passing that Catherine, her daughter-in-law, had recently decided to create a family scrapbook and had asked Bronwyn if she had any old photographs to contribute to the project. She was intending to present it to Taylor on his next birthday, three months hence.

"I've got boxes of photos," Bronwyn confessed. "I don't know where to begin to choose which ones to give her. Would you take a few minutes and look through some of them with me and give me your suggestions?"

"Sure," Janet nodded. "I used to do a bit of scrapbooking back in Canada and enjoyed it. I've got boxes of photos myself that need to be organized and put in albums. Maybe this will inspire me to get going."

Janet followed Bronwyn into the dining room where several open boxes were spread across the table. A few piles of assorted pictures were haphazardly scattered in front of the boxes. Bronwyn rifled through them and pulled out three photos of Taylor as a small child.

"He was so cute," she said softly, as if to herself, then turned to Janet and added, "I don't think I've ever told you this, but we adopted Taylor. Philip and I tried to have children for several years, but to no avail. Finally we gave up. A good friend of ours worked at an adoption agency. She helped us."

Janet swallowed before replying, "Did it take...a long time?" she asked haltingly.

"Well, yes, it was...it was a bit complicated." She paused, then her mood brightened and she went on, "He was only a month old when we got him—just a wee one," she smiled at the memory.

"Umm," Janet murmured. "I've, uh, heard it's best for the child to be placed as young as possible," she added.

"I think so," Bronwyn continued. "He was such a good baby. Mind you, we had some challenges when he was in school, but look at him now. I must confess—I'm very proud of him."

"And so you should be," Janet agreed. "He's a very fine young man with a beautiful family."

Bronwyn pulled out more photos and in minutes had more than forty of them spread across the table. She and Janet pored over them and finally chose eighteen and put them aside for Catherine: Taylor alone, Taylor with Philip, Taylor with Philip and Bronwyn, Taylor at various ages. Catherine would have a variety to work with in developing her scrapbook.

Janet picked up one of the photos not included in the pile for Catherine. She looked into the eyes of a smiling five-year-old Taylor, standing on a rock wall by the seashore. He was grinning and even at such a young age, she thought to herself, he looked remarkably like Brian. She put the photo down quickly and shook her head, as if to throw off the thought. Bronwyn didn't notice.

Weeks went by. Bronwyn never mentioned Catherine's scrapbook or the adoption issue again. Janet thought about it occasionally but had decided she would not bring it up, though she would have loved to ask a few questions. *If it's meant to be*, she reminded herself, *it will be.*

Cecilia completed her Chef's Course and loved it so much, she decided to enroll in the Advanced Course which would begin a month later. To celebrate her graduation, she hosted another dinner party. Carmela, Paula Jean and Janet, along with Bronwyn and Eleanor, gathered in Cecilia's kitchen the day before and she put them all to work. Eleanor teased that Cecilia was putting them all through chef's school!

Cecilia decided to invite Tom and Jennifer as well as Taylor and Catherine to the dinner party. Stephanie, whose visits from New York were becoming more frequent, was in town and offered to take all the children to a Disney movie that was playing in Florence. She had become quite attached to both the Broderick and the Bradshaw children, all of whom affectionately called her "Auntie Stephanie". Eleanor teased that she wasn't sure anymore if Stephanie's regular jaunts across the Atlantic meant she missed her mother–or her 'nieces and nephews'.

When they arrived the following evening, Taylor and Catherine brought expensive Italian wine and Tom and Jennifer carried in a magnificent bouquet of white and yellow roses. Both couples chimed "Congratulations, Chef Cecilia!" and hugged her warmly.

The dinner party was an even greater success than the first one. Cecilia beamed with pleasure at each 'ooh' and 'aah' of her guests. She would never have believed she could have so much fun cooking and feeding her friends and family. Eleanor remarked that her sister looked ten years younger since she'd embarked on her food career.

Paula Jean, though she enjoyed the art course, decided once was enough and instead, tried her hand at writing. She told Carmela one day that she thought her experience with Ferko was good material for a novel. Carmela promptly declared, "So write one already!"

"Me?" Paula Jean raised an eyebrow. "I was thinking I'd try to find someone else, like a real writer, to pick up the idea."

"Why?" the always practically minded Carmela questioned. "You're the one who lived it. You experienced it. You can write the story like no one else can."

"But I've never written anything but letters," Paula Jean protested.

"So write me a letter all about Ferko," Carmela wouldn't let her off the hook. " A really long one. Embellish the story here and there. Let your imagination lead you. Come on, you can do it!"

Reluctantly at first, Paula Jean began writing in a simple notebook. After a few weeks, she admitted to Carmela, "This is getting to be fun. The more I write, the more I want to write. I'm getting all kinds of ideas and sometimes I feel like the story is running ahead of me."

Carmela grinned. "Told you you could do it."

The 'Tuscany Golden Girls' gathered at Café Toscana the following week and by request of the group who had by now learned that Paula Jean was writing a novel about what they all called the 'Ferko affair', she brought the first two chapters along and distributed copies to each of them, now a group of six: Carmela, Janet, Paula Jean, Cecilia, Eleanor and Bronwyn. Paula Jean was taken aback when all of them, without exception, delved into the printed pages as soon as they'd given their order to Carlo, their regular waiter. She giggled quietly as she thought, *Never have we sat around this table and been so quiet!*

Janet was the first to finish reading and looking up at Paula Jean, exclaimed, "Brilliant! I love it!" One by one, the others added their accolades and voted unanimously that Paula Jean should keep writing, finish the novel and plan on becoming a best selling author.

"Oh, come on," she protested. "I think y'all are getting a bit carried away." Despite the fact that she'd been in Italy a few years by now, the southern lady never lost her penchant for saying 'y'all'.

Eleanor spoke up. "Listen, Paula Jean, I am very serious when I say this. You have a real gift for writing. Your use of words, your expressions, the way you put the story together–it's really, really good. Don't sell yourself short. I think you've uncovered a talent you apparently haven't used before. It's never too late, you know."

The earnestness with which Eleanor made her remarks gave pause to Paula Jean's reticence. Cecilia and Carmela added their encouragement to Eleanor's and Bronwyn, the shy member of the group, finally spoke up and said, "A few years ago, I worked at a publishing house in Essex. Your writing really is excellent."

All eyes turned in her direction. "Really?" Janet was the first to speak. "I never knew that about you."

Bronwyn blushed. "It was a long time ago but it was my favorite job. I got paid to read manuscripts that were submitted for publication. I love to read–and to get paid for it besides was just lovely." She turned back toward Paula Jean, "I really meant what I said. You should keep writing."

"Uh, thank you." Paula Jean was a bit overwhelmed with all the support that had been voiced.

That evening Janet remembered that she hadn't checked her mailbox when she and Bronwyn returned from the city, so she walked out to the end of her driveway. Pulling out a few envelopes and two magazines, she flipped through them as she made her way back to the open front door. One of the pieces of mail, in fact, was not hers but had been mistakenly delivered to her box. It was actually addressed to Bronwyn. She dropped her mail on the front hall table, and slipped back out to take the letter next door.

"Come on in," Bronwyn called when she heard Janet call out, "Hello." Bronwyn came into the living room carrying a parcel of some kind, took the letter Janet offered her and asked her if she'd like some tea.

"Why not?" Janet replied. "It's still early."

"Good," Bronwyn remarked, as she put the parcel down on the coffee table and went into the kitchen. Janet followed her, chose her tea bag from Bronwyn's ever present mahogany Tea Box, and slid into one of the kitchen chairs.

"It's timely that you just popped in," Bronwyn said, as she poured water over the tea bag. "I was just thinking about you."

"Hope it was good," Janet grinned.

"Of course," Bronwyn smiled back. "Here, have a cookie."

"No thanks. Just the tea is fine. I'm still digesting the cannolis!"

Bronwyn laughed, then assumed a more serious expression. "May I tell you something?"

"Of course!" Janet looked up.

"Just a minute," Bronwyn said as she darted into the living room and returned quickly with the parcel she'd left on the coffee table in her hand.

"Not a soul knows about this. I never even told Philip, may he rest in peace."

She paused, then pulled a thick stack of papers out of what Janet now realized was a large, padded manila envelope.

"There's about 300 pages here of something I wrote some years ago. I've never shown it to anyone, but after our talking with Paula Jean today about her novel, I started thinking about this manuscript that's been stuffed away in my closet for years. Just before you came over, I was wondering whether I should ask you to read it and lo and behold, you show up at the door."

"With pleasure," Janet replied, a bit surprised. "What's it about?"

"Well," Bronwyn leaned back in her chair and sighed, "it's also a novel and I suppose bears some resemblance in part to what Paula Jean is doing. This is also based in fact but not nearly as much fact as Paula Jean has to work with. I just....well, I...let me give you the background."

Janet nodded, "I'm all ears."

"A few weeks ago I told you that Taylor was adopted, remember?"

Janet's stomach lurched and knotted, as she said, "Yes, I remember."

"When Philip and I decided we would adopt a child, I wrote a letter to a school friend of mine who had emigrated to Canada." Janet suppressed the urge to gasp aloud when she heard the word 'Canada'.

"We were best of friends growing up" Bronwyn was saying, oblivious to Janet's growing distress, "and we'd kept in touch. I knew she worked for an international adoption agency, so I wrote her asking for advice. We corresponded a bit back and forth and a few months later, she called me one day. I was shocked to hear her voice at the other end of the line. 'Bronwyn', she said to me, 'are you and Philip ready for a baby?'

"Well, I was aghast. 'Why', I said. 'What do you mean?' She told me that the agency had a baby boy in need of a home and although it was a bit of an unusual case, she couldn't get Philip and me out of her mind so she'd already gone to her Director and asked if she could discuss this particular baby with us. She kept saying to me, 'Bronwyn, I just feel like this baby should be yours.'

"The Director approved her request and told her to phone us. I called Philip from the other room. We had just a few minutes to decide. It was all so sudden, yet we'd been waiting for a child for so long so Philip looked at me and said, 'Let's do it.' I got back on the phone with my friend and told her we'd take the baby and was about to ask her about arrangements when she interrupted me and said, 'I'm flying to London in five days time. I'll bring the baby to you. The authorizations are all prepared already. I'll explain everything to you when I get there. By the way, he'll be one month old the day I arrive in London and he's a darling little boy. I'm just so sure he's meant for you.'

Silent tears were slowly trickling down Janet's face when Bronwyn looked directly at her. "I know," she said quietly, "it's a moving story. I get teary-eyed myself when I think about it, even after all these years." She reached across the table and squeezed Janet's hand. Janet inhaled deeply but said nothing.

Bronwyn continued, "When my friend arrived with the baby–it was Taylor, of course–she brought several documents, including some which she said are not normally given to adoptive parents but she explained why. Taylor's mother had died from complications after child birth, my friend told me, and his father, still quite young at the time, was devastated and felt he couldn't care for the child without his wife. The family traced their lineage back to Britain and therefore, the baby's father asked if it were possible, he would like his son to be raised by a British couple, preferably in England, rather than in Canada."

Bronwyn breathed a deep, long sigh, then looked at Janet. "I–we–were so thrilled to have a baby, Janet, but at the same time, I had a strange reaction. I wept on and off for several days over the circumstances of how we got Taylor. Philip thought I was overdoing it, but I kept thinking about this poor young girl who died–so young–and the young father.....I couldn't stop thinking about them...the pain... the despair he must have experienced....I don't know, Janet, it just gripped me.

Janet was weeping openly now.

"So I decided after a few weeks, that I needed to write the story and keep it for Taylor when he grew up. I wrote it as a novel because I just had the bare facts about his parents, but I've never given it to him. I never did anything with it, in fact."

She lifted the manuscript and held it out to Janet. "Would you be willing...I'd like to what you think of...."

Janet raised her hand to interrupt her and said, "Just a minute. I'll be right back." With that, she flew out the door, ran across the driveway and into her home. With trembling hands, she grabbed Julie and Brian's wedding album from her bookshelf and ran back into Bronwyn's home.

Bronwyn looked up startled as Janet put the album down on the table. Composing herself, Janet said, "Bronwyn, I need to show you something."

Slowly, she opened the album cover and slid it across the table, turning it to face in the right direction so Bronwyn could see the photo correctly.

Brownyn looked down. She stared at the wedding picture, looked up at Janet, a look of total confusion on her face, then looked back at the photograph.

"Who...who is this?" Bronwyn asked very slowly.

Janet gulped. "That's my sister's wedding portrait."

"Your.....sister? You never mentioned a... sister....." she stopped and looked intently at Janet. Then she looked again at the photo, clearly focusing on Brian.

Bronwyn was silent for several minutes, just staring at the handsome young groom. Then she closed her eyes and sat perfectly still. Janet waited, apprehensive.

Finally Bronwyn opened her eyes and looked at Janet. "Your sister's husband–what was his name?"

"Brian–Brian Butler."

"Oh, God..." Bronwyn covered her face with her hands and leaned forward on the table. Janet tensed. Perhaps she'd been wrong to show her the album. *I was too impulsive*, she berated herself.

"Bronwyn, I'm so sorry. I didn't mean to upset you. I'm sorry..."

Bronwyn looked up, her face as white as a new fallen snow. She reached across the table and took both of Janet's hands in hers. "No, no, no. No need to be sorry. No, it's...it's just a shock. I'm...I'm stunned. No, no, no need to apologize," she repeated almost in a whisper.

Janet squirmed in the chair. She didn't know what to do.

Bronwyn sat back, letting go of Janet's hands. After another extended silence, she looked pleadingly at Janet. "Tell me about your sister," she said, gesturing towards the album.

For the next few minutes, Janet told Bronwyn all about Julie, the difficult pregnancy, how she had died during the night after her baby was born, how Janet and Carl had made the trip to Toronto, the trauma of learning that Brian had decided to give the baby away before they even got there to see him, Julie's funeral and how they'd lost touch with Brian ever since.

Then she told Bronwyn about the first time she saw Taylor walking down the street with another man and it had stopped her in her tracks. She related how she'd pulled out all the boxes she'd stored in her attic, looking for Julie's medical records, trying to piece things together after she'd met Taylor in person–all because he looked just like Brian had at his age. She acknowledged her doubts, her disbelief that it could actually be so, yet how she hadn't been able to shake her conviction that Taylor must be her sister's son.

When she finished, Bronwyn's tears flowed freely as she asked, "How did you keep this inside all this time?"

Janet confessed that she'd talked with Carmela, and that Jennifer had noticed her reaction when Taylor came to the dinner party and had asked her about it.

"So Tom and Jennifer know?" Bronwyn asked, calmly.

Janet nodded, hesitantly. "Well, they know what I've thought. They ... they saw the wedding album and..."

Bronwyn whispered, "Then they know. Who could deny it?" She looked back at the photo. "He's as handsome as his father was–maybe a little more," she said, just like a proud mother would. Another prolonged silence as Bronwyn looked through the entire wedding album, page by page, slowly, deliberately.

When she finished, she looked up at Janet and said, "What do we do now?"

"I...I was hoping you would know what to do," Janet replied.

Bronwyn stood up. "I really need a cup of tea. How about you?" Janet nodded and Brownyn disappeared into the kitchen.

Utter turmoil didn't begin to describe Janet's feelings, but she didn't have long to deal with them. Bronwyn re-entered the dining room with two mugs of tea, sat down and sighed again. Then lifting her eyes to meet Janet's, she smiled–– a warm smile that melted the tension.

"Janet, I was raised to believe that everything happens for a reason; that somehow in God's mysterious ways, He is involved in the paths we take through life. Somehow it's all for our good. I don't pretend to understand it all, but I was raised to believe it and I do."

She tilted her head to one side, reached across the table to clasp Janet's hand and continued, "But though I've always believed that, I have to tell you that what just happened here at my table is far beyond anything I could ever have imagined that God would do."

Janet's eyes had been glued to Bronwyn's face as she spoke. When she paused, Janet gave a slight nod but said nothing.

"I can't think of anyone nicer to be Taylor's aunt," Bronwyn said in a soft voice.

Janet dissolved into tears. Bronwyn got up from her chair, walked around the table and lifted Janet into a warm embrace. When she could speak again, Janet pulled back slightly, and with a tear-stained face, said to Bronwyn, "And I can't think of anyone nicer to have raised my nephew into the amazing young man that he is. Thank you."

They talked for another hour. The implications of their newly discovered relationship were a bit overwhelming, to say the least. Bronwyn and Janet each put forth various scenarios for telling Taylor but rejected one after the other.

Finally Janet said very sensibly, "Bronwyn, we're not going to come up with a good plan right now. It's too soon. You and I have to process what just happened."

Bronwyn smiled, "You're so right. I was getting a bit carried away, wasn't I?"

"We both were, my friend," Janet replied. "What do you think of this? Our group is meeting for lunch on Thursday. That gives you and me three days to recover from this morning. If you think you're ready by then, why don't we share this news with our friends after lunch and get their input. There's a wealth of wisdom and experience among our ladies. Someone will have the stroke of insight we need. What do you think?"

"Brilliant!" Bronwyn smiled broadly. "That's brilliant. Let's do it."

Lunch was scheduled at Carmela's that Thursday. She had been promising the women an authentic Mexican feast and they were all anticipating the experience. Cecilia had confided to Eleanor that she hoped the food wouldn't be too hot. "I don't know if my British palate can take it!" she giggled.

Everyone arrived a bit early and by pre-arrangement, they had all decided to wear their brightest, most colorful outfits to add to the festive mood of the day. Carmela laughed out loud when she saw them all trooping in her front door.

"You're not eager, are you?" she taunted them. "Wow–you look like a Mexican dance troupe," she chuckled. She waved them through the house and out onto the patio which she had decorated with paper lanterns and colorful tablecloths and napkins.

Carmela had prepared Chile Rellenos in tomato sauce from her own recipe, handed down from her mother. She also served Mexican rice and refried beans with fresh corn tortillas she made by hand. Generous pitchers of homemade lemonade were replenished as needed. The food was plentiful and so was the conversation. Carmela asked Paula Jean how the novel was coming and Cecilia had new stories to tell from her Advanced Chef's Course.

They had just cleared the tables and settled themselves for Mexican style coffee and churros to top off the meal, when Bronwyn glanced at Janet and then cleared her throat.

Looking around the table she began. "Even though I haven't been here too long, I just want to say that this group is the best circle of friends I've ever had in my life."

They all smiled in return and Paula Jean interjected, "We're so happy you've become a part of us, Bronwyn."

"Thank you," she acknowledged, and continued. "I know some of you have shared personal stories with each other before I came here."

She paused, looked again at Janet who nodded slightly. Everyone's attention was on Bronwyn.

She took a deep breath and began, "Today, if it's OK with you, I have a story I'd like to tell. It all began with a phone call...."

Pizza and Promises

Teasers from the sequel to Pasta, Poppy Fields and Pearls

From her kitchen window, Janet noticed the strangers approaching Bronwyn's front door. Something about them gave her an uneasy feeling...

Taylor's forty-first birthday was four days away and the scrapbook still wasn't finished....

"It's Casey," Catherine cried into the phone. "There's been an accident...come quickly..."

"I'm going to find him," Taylor said with a grim, determined look. "I want to ask him why. Why?" His voice was tinged with bitterness.

Carmela and Paula Jean stayed with Cecilia day and night for nearly three weeks....

"Where is she?" Eleanor cried out in anguish. "Why can't I reach her?"

Coming soon... You won't want to miss it!

23643601R00100

Made in the USA
Charleston, SC
31 October 2013